GW00391433

GENESIS

HAZEL LONGUET

Novel Experience

Novel Experience

A Novel Experience book.
First published in Great Britain in 2019 by Novel Experience

Cover design by Hazel Longuet

Edited by Rosebud Editing
www.rosebudediting.com

www.hazellonguet.com

To Gill and Derek Longuet.

As with everything in life, this is a work of collaboration. Without my parents' support and undying faith in me, I would not have seen this book through to completion. So, for all the meals, the gardening, the dog walks, and the absolute faith, I dedicate this book to them.

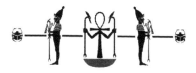

THE SEER

The fountain of knowledge was bathed in sunshine, the water throwing glimmering lights around the walls of the courtyard. The fountain held centre stage, with four twisted old olive trees standing sentry in each quadrant of the famed courtyard of all knowledge. Except for the gentle trills of the dancing water and the distant birdsong from the gardens surrounding the temple complex, all was quiet. The day was young and the sun yet soft.

Kiya hummed softly whilst gazing into her scrying mirror. At only one and twenty years, she was young for her weighty role, yet everyone agreed that never had a pharaoh been so blessed with such a powerful and accurate seer.

Raiders had captured her family long ago and sold them into slavery. They were split amongst various owners and spread across the known world. Kiya considered herself one of the lucky ones to have found her way to the pharaoh's court.

When she'd come into her powers as a mere child of eight, the pharaoh's court considered her something of a child protégé. Her astounding accuracy saw her fly up the ranks until she'd taken the role of Pharaoh's Seer. She'd held the position for five years and, so far, had never seen something that didn't come to pass.

The early mornings were her favourite time, when the sun had yet to heat the air, the temple was wrapped in the silence of sleeping priests, and the birds were rejoicing in the dawning of a new day. She could let her mind wander and enjoy a modicum of freedom before her duties pressed down on her.

She laid the mirror down with great care and wandered over to sit on the edge of the fountain, trailing her fingers through the twirling jets. The sun played with her honey-blonde hair, bringing fiery highlights into focus.

A movement in the water caught her eye, and she stared, immediately taken into a vision. As the importance of this vision became obvious, she held her breath, wishing that this was the prophecy that broke her perfect record. Unable to process what she'd seen, she hurried back to the scrying mirror that rested on one of the devotional cushions scattered across the yard. She gazed into the depths of the polished metal surface, which clouded and again replayed the same vision, with the same details and same horrific outcome.

Dropping her precious mirror, she lifted the long, white lengths of her dress and ran to gain the high priest's counsel. Telling the pharaoh what she'd seen could result in her own execution. Only the high priest could help her. She knew this emphatically, for the vision had shown her the path to take.

The future never lied.

THE HIGH PRIEST

Haremakhet was particularly reflective that morning. Egypt had basked in a prolonged period of peace under the guiding hand of the pharaoh and his oracle. As a high priest, it had been a period of great reward. Less political wrangling gave him time to build the temple's brethren. He'd opened religious studies to more of his pharaoh's subjects. They lived in blessed times, a golden epoch.

And yet, today was different. Today, he felt the dark hand of fate hovering.

He swept the Holy of Holies with a worn broom almost bare of bristles. His assistant priests had tried to wrestle it from his hands more times than he cared to remember, and yet, he always returned to it. It wasn't his responsibility to clean the inner sanctums anymore—it hadn't been for years —but he felt closest to his gods when he was toiling in manual labour, serving their needs. It was a philosophy he insisted all his priests follow, but few embraced it as whole-heartedly as he.

He heard the soft tap of feet running through the

temple, toward him. Surprised another was about so early, he turned to greet his visitor. He knew it was Kiya as the sun lit her fiery hair, which was so unusual within the dominion. She was trying to show respect to the deities but was obviously in distress as she hurried through the rituals to get to him.

"Your Eminence," she said, flowing into a deep curtsy, her left arm across her chest as she bowed her head and bent at the waist.

"Your Omniscience," he replied formally, touching his head and heart and bowing back. "You appear in a rush, my dear. Is all well with you?"

"With me, yes. But not with our world, Haremakhet. The gods, praise be to them, presented me with a vision of such consequence that I fear our society is doomed," Kiya said. She looked earnestly at the high priest. "I seek your counsel, Haremakhet, for this is a prophecy of such import, yet I can't share it with our great pharaoh. The gods forbid it, and even if it were not so, I would be extremely fearful to report such loathsome news. He would surely kill me to remove the blight."

Haremakhet had never seen Kiya so riled. She was always the epitome of decorum and propriety. A woman of rare beauty, beguiling and serene. Her greatest quality was how unaware she was of her impact on others. As High Seer, she was destined to remain a maiden, her virtue intact. Only if it were so would the gods continue to bless her future visions. He'd often thought it sad but acknowledged the importance of her role to the entire Egyptian dominion.

"Do the gods, praise be to them, sanction my consultation, Kiya?"

She raised her cornflower blue eyes, eyes so startling and intense that people often had difficulty looking at her.

"Haremakhet, they demand it. The actions you and I take today will shake the world over three thousand years after we meet our makers. This is our destiny—to set theirs."

"Whose, Kiya?" he asked, bewildered by her trance-like reply.

"The House of Scarabs, Haremakhet. The Resurrectionists. Those we choose today will carry the secrets of resurrection forward to allow our great pharaohs to rise again. They must leave our lands and travel to new, unknown territories and carry that knowledge, protecting it until the time is right to start again. Our great gods will wither, and a new god will rise and be worshipped around the world. The ways of our people will be forgotten, lost to the desert sands. Our great knowledge will be lost, and civilisation will retreat, leaving our people illiterate and backward.

"Egypt will lose its place in the global theatre. Our temples will be looted as the people turn to their new god, a god so great that he has no name. His followers will banish the other gods into the realms of myth and legend. Such is our future, High Priest, and there is no action I can recommend to change it. It is set and will happen. All I can do is guide you to ensure we respect the desires of our pharaohs, past and present, and give them the gift of regeneration. This is what we must do."

He stared at her as her words resonated in the echoes of the Holy of Holies. He said nothing. He wanted to. He wanted to shout at the gods for abandoning them to such a bleak future, for not fighting this all-powerful usurper. Yet, he knew that they were all-seeing and all-knowing. This abandonment, whilst extreme, must surely be for some long-term benefit that was too great for him to imagine.

"Kiya, the rituals of resurrection take twenty years to

master, and only a few of the graduates are ever granted the powers by the gods. Every one of them is known and would be missed. How can we create this House of Scarabs without showing our hand?"

"My dear friend," she whispered, grasping his arm, "the gods will preside over the initiation. They will seed a latent talent that negates the need for years of apprenticeship. We must select the candidates from the brotherhood of priests that serve Khepri, Bastet, and Sobek. I know not why. We must make haste. Our preparations can't take long. The selection must be completed within two full moons. Blessings be, Haremakhet. Tell no one of this, for if we fail, our souls will be subjected to the rage of Anubis in the afterlife."

"Wait. Kiya, I have so many questions."

Kiya smiled. "As do I, Your Eminence, but we have all the information deemed necessary by the gods to complete our task."

Her eyes glazed as she gazed into the distant corner of the holies. She shook her head slightly and turned back to him.

"Haremakhet, our son. You will live out a long and peaceful life serving us, as will more generations to come. Our demise is assured but not in your lifetime and not permanently—if you do as we request. Be good and be true. Offer wise counsel. You will bathe in our love."

Kiya's eyes cleared as she found his gaze. "It's time, Your Eminence," she said with a gesticulation of piety.

Touching his head and heart and bowing from the waist, he answered, "It appears it is, Your Omniscience. Gods' blessings go with you."

Kiya backed out of the Holies before rushing away.

The high priest studied the floor, watching a scarab

beetle dart across the sandy surface. The light played on its back, turning the black body into an oiled sheen of purple, green, and blue. He closed his eyes and contemplated everything Kiya had shared with him. With a deep sigh, he picked up the broom and completed the temple floor, said his morning prayers in a whisper, and left to convene a religious council.

CALLING THE CONGRESS

"I do not understand, Haremakhet. How can we take the priests away from their temples? Who will hold the devotionals and lead the worship? We've never done this."

Haremakhet smiled gently at his deputy high priest. Pabasa had always been a traditionalist and struggled with change. He was a good man, a great orator, and thrived within a controlled environment. But he lacked the vision Haremakhet brought to the role. Every change Haremakhet initiated resulted in heated debate and long discourse, which invariably ended in a more rounded and considered approach. They were an odd couple, where the mass of the whole far exceeded the merits of the two individuals.

"I know, Pabasa. We shall indeed face trials, as you so eloquently indicated, but bringing the priests together will enable great theological debate. I believe we'll uncover some hidden gems. It's an opportunity for us to open our minds to the future of our faith without the heavy encumbrance of our priestly duties. We must look to the gods for direction, and through their greatness, ideas will flow."

"I don't like it," puffed Pabasa. He was a man that liked his food, which was reflected in his solid build and mottled nose. When he smiled, his chestnut eyes twinkled with merriment. He was everyone's favourite blustering uncle, the one who would help anyone but grumble under his breath as he did so. He was a man upon whom people could rely.

"Trust me, my friend, and organise messengers to inform the priests. We will start with those of Sobek, Bastet, and Khepri as a trial. If the meetings proceed as I hope they will, we can include the other priesthoods later. That way, I can reassure you before we disrupt every temple across the land."

"I suppose a trial makes sense," agreed Pabasa as he bowed and left the room.

Haremakhet rubbed his head. *At least we might also get some merit from calling the priests together, other than finding the three candidates Kiya requires,* he thought. He was growing to like the idea of the meeting the more he considered it.

The congress was set for four weeks later, to allow the priests to arrange cover and travel to Thebes.

Kiya's days dragged. The pharaoh planned his activities around her daily updates, yet she had none. Since that first vision, she hadn't a single new prophecy, just the same one on repeat.

She saw the downfall of the Egyptian dominion. The rise of the one true god. The empty husks of the pharaohs, barren and displayed like sideshow exhibits. She saw the

House of Scarabs running throughout time, holders of a great secret. She saw the moment they helped the great, all-powerful pharaohs to live again. All this, she saw but nothing else. She had no news to share with the pharaoh.

After a week of desperate scrying and praying for her normal visions to return, she'd noticed people following her around the temple and palace, monitoring her. She suspected the pharaoh was having her watched. She'd considered fabricating stories to placate him but knew when they didn't come to pass, he'd guess the truth. She prayed that once they'd selected the members for the House of Scarabs, her revelations would return. A High Seer with no visions added no value beyond that of the flesh, which was not a path she wanted to explore.

***

Pabasa had organised the council with military-like precision. He ordered the construction of a canvas village in the temple's courtyard, next to the holy lake, in which he planned to house the priests. He'd ordered provisions to ensure it would be an event they would remember. The pharaoh had graciously sent his campaign kitchens to assist the temple cooks, and Pabasa had enjoyed the menu sampling as he selected the meals for each day. Never one to live moderately, when he could feast, he overindulged and suffered for a couple of days.

Few had ever been to the Karnak temple, and even fewer were likely to see it again, so he wanted to ensure he presented it in perfect form. He'd ordered the initiates to clean and polish every surface. The lamps glittered, beams flaring on the metal surfaces excavated from beneath years of soot and wax. Pabasa may not agree with the concept behind the council, but he was determined to prove Haremakhet's faith in him was well-placed.

Amongst this maelstrom of activity, Haremakhet prayed. He meditated on the future Kiya had painted in such devastating detail. He struggled with doing nothing to prevent it coming to pass. It felt remiss, a dereliction of his duties, and yet, it was a gods-sent message. He was duty-bound to obey it.

The conflict made him yearn for the simple certainty in his faith he'd always enjoyed. Now that absolute faith had a vast chasm running through it. He felt his efforts were best spent contemplating his religious convictions. Pabasa was infinitely better at managing the logistics of the event, so Haremakhet pondered the religious agendas—both the council's and that of the House of Scarabs.

The days passed.

The scrying mirror remained blank, as it had for weeks. Kiya cleansed it in the holy water, hoping the gods' blessings may restore its strength and vigour. She tipped the silver jug, pouring a wash of water across the entire pane before placing it in the sun to allow the god Ra to dry it in his bright rays.

Kiya sighed. It had been hard facing the pharaoh each day to admit her vision had failed again. She was used to being a valued adviser. Her presence had always warmed the pharaoh's smile, and so, he'd granted her privileges that far outranked her position as a foreign slave. Now she knew that position weakened. The pharaoh was becoming enraged as days and weeks passed with no word from the gods, no clear directions for him to follow. She understood his frustration but could do nothing to restore her second sight.

The fountains trickled, adding music to the afternoon air. Kiya stared into the deep pools at their base, looking for inspiration. She was so lost in thought, she didn't hear the gentle tap of Haremakhet's sandals on the dusty stone path and looked up in shock when he placed his hand on her shoulder.

"Sorry, Kiya. I didn't mean to startle you. Your thoughts look heavy, my child. Is there anything with which I can help you?"

She smiled, shaking her head, "I was contemplating the loss of my visions. The pharaoh's wrath grows stronger every day. I fear what will happen if they don't return soon. I am already being watched," she said, nodding towards a temple gardener who was watching them with little discretion. "I'm aware some of my predecessors used their knowledge for personal gain, so I understand his trepidation, but it pains me after these long years of dedicated service." She sighed, looking down into the waters one last time before standing. "Come, Your Eminence. Let us walk next to the great lake, where our conversation can be shrouded in privacy."

Haremakhet gestured for her to lead the way. They chatted about temple politics as they strolled past the gardener.

It was one of those rare days when the gods had blessed Egypt with a breeze that lifted the scorching weather, giving the people respite from the furnace-like temperature of summer. Kiya carried a parasol to protect her pale skin, gifted by the pharaoh after a particularly fruitful vision.

The holy lake sat to the side of the main temple

complex. It had long been Kiya's favourite spot to spend her hours in meditation and prayer. The large rectangular lake had gently pitched steps leading down into the water. Palm trees provided valuable shade around its perimeter.

As they ambled around the lake, Haremakhet chatted. Kiya turned to him, raising her eyebrows quizzically. "My friend, enough of your benign chatter. Voice your request. It's most unlike you to skirt a subject so, and I'm finding it disconcerting," she said.

"Your visions have returned?" he asked.

"No, Your Eminence. Your waffling gave me enough clarity to make an educated guess," she said, patting his arm and smiling.

Haremakhet smiled down at her, nodding his head ruefully.

"I've been thinking, and I've concluded that I need you to help me select the members for this mission. Despite much thought and prayer on the subject, I am no closer to understanding the selection of the members of this group. What attributes do they require—well, aside from the logical need for intelligence, piety, and the willingness to put aside family and country for the protection of their beliefs?" He stopped and turned back towards the temple, gesturing with his hand. "How do I check their piety without revealing the task? It troubles me. This is a heavy duty, and we only have one chance to succeed. I wish your help, Kiya. Will you attend and assist me in the identification of our candidates?"

She nodded and smiled at some junior priests who walked past them, watching them walk into the distance before turning to reply to Haremakhet. "I'm happy to, but whether the gods will answer our calls and provide guidance is as yet unassured." She slipped her hand through the crook of his arm and said, "Let's continue our prayers as we walk on this fine day."

YUYA

"Your Eminence, a messenger has arrived from the pharaoh's high priest of Karnak. He's requested an audience with you. He says it's of the greatest importance. Shall I bring him in to you?"

Yuya looked up from his weaving. He carefully placed the shuttle on the loom's shelf before standing and brushing himself down.

"Of course, my dear friend. Please do. Can you arrange refreshments? The poor chap must be weary from such a long and tiresome journey."

Yuya looked around the humble room he used for his daily activities before hurrying to tidy away the clutter of life. It wasn't every day he had such an illustrious visitor. A representative of the high priest of Karnak should be treated with the greatest courtesy and respect.

He moved two large floor cushions next to the low side table and fussed with organising the room until his apostle returned with the messenger. The poor man looked worn down from his trip. His long robes echoed the colour of the desert sand through which he'd struggled to reach this forlorn outpost in the Southern desert.

"Oh, my dear man, come and rest. Please take a seat. Ahmes, hurry with the refreshments, if you'd please." He turned back to the messenger, who'd sunk gratefully onto the deep cushion. "I am Yuya, High Priest of this temple. I believe you bear a message for me."

The messenger struggled to stand again, but Yuya sank to the cushion next to him and gestured for him to remain seated.

"Your Eminence, I am Bebi, a messenger of Haremakhet. I beg you to forgive my appearance. It has been a long and difficult journey, and I fear our god Shu was at work, for I encountered two large sandstorms."

Yuya nodded. "Yes, Shu is active at this time of the year. Still, his bountiful grace spreads the plants' seeds and helps life to continue, so we thank him for his efforts. Welcome to our temple, Bebi, messenger of Haremakhet. The great gods Khepri and Montu open our temple's doors to you."

Yuya turned as Ahmes returned with a tray of fresh juice and plump dates.

"Thank you for your speed, Ahmes. I fear our guest has suffered much at the hands of the wind god on his journey to our remote temple." He gestured to the heavily laden tray that Ahmes had placed on the side table. "Please eat and drink a little before you share your news."

Yuya watched Bebi drink the glass empty in one gulp before stuffing dates into his mouth in earnest. With a smile, he said, "Ahmes, please prepare a meal for our honoured guest."

"Forgive me, Your Eminence, but I lost my rations in the storm two days past, and I've had no food since. I saved my water supply, but it got low as the storms delayed me considerably, so I've been on quarter rations. The gods will reward your generosity. Of that, I'm sure."

"No apologies required, Bebi, messenger of Haremakhet. I fully understand the trials of journeying to our temple. Few try, and those who do rarely fare as well as you have. My predecessor told me that our dear temple is the farthest from any settlement in the pharaoh's great domain and the deepest into the deserts. Whether this be truth or speculation, I know not, but it wouldn't surprise me if it were so. Our provision supply can be rather sketchy, so Ahmes and I farm the oasis land. Whilst we aren't quite self-sufficient, with hard work, we can survive several months on the fruits of our labours. Our gods truly bless us."

Yuya studied Bebi. The bright blue eyes against a skin so dark hinted at a mixed heritage. The tribes to the Northwest of the dominion had piercing blue eyes such as his, but it was rare to see them so far south, and rarely was their skin as richly toned as his. He must have been five and twenty years old. Long journeys under the sun and sands' destructive forces had hewn his face, so he looked older. Dark shadows circled his eyes, and tiredness dragged down at his mouth.

Bebi drank three glasses of juice and finished the dates before using the damp cloth Ahmes had thoughtfully supplied to cleanse his hands and face. "I feel as if I've feasted. Thank you, sir. Now I must get to the reason for my journey."

Yuya inclined his head and smiled his agreement.

"The pharaoh's own High Priest of Karnak has entrusted me to deliver an invitation to the esteemed High Priest of Yabaktari. His Eminence Yuya, can I trust that you are he?"

Yuya bowed from the waist and, with his hand on his

heart, said, "I am Yuya, High Priest of Yabaktari, as deemed by the gods Khepri and Montu and signed by His Eminence Haremakhet, Royal High Priest of Karnak. As I bear witness before the gods, I am he."

Bebi nodded, "His Eminence Haremakhet requests your presence at a religious congress in Karnak. It is scheduled to commence by the light of the next full moon. He is gathering all the high priests of Khepri, Sobek, and Bastet to convene a religious retreat in which he will guide a discussion on the theology and practises of your houses and to explore how to deliver the messages of the gods to more of our dear Pharaoh's subjects. They hold this meeting under the auspices of our great Pharaoh. He trusts you will make haste to Karnak forthwith. May the gods' blessings be upon you, High Priest Yuya of Yabaktari." Bebi fell into a deep bow with his arm across his chest, hand on heart, and head bent low.

Yuya placed his hand upon the man's head, and Bebi rose to his full towering height. He was a full head higher than Yuya, who was not an insignificant height himself.

"This news is perplexing. I have never heard of such an event. There are only two of us here. Who will undertake the rituals? I cannot leave Ahmes here on his own. Were he to fall ill, there would be no one to care for him. Yet, I can't refuse to attend if it's under the auspices of the pharaoh. Hmm... I must give this some thought."

Bebi had poured himself another glass of juice as he listened to Yuya mulling the issue over. "His Eminence Haremakhet predicted this issue may occur for the smaller, outlying temples. Thus, he sent members of his own priesthood as messengers. I passed my merits last year and am now a fully practising member of the priesthood, although yet to select my final gods. So, I can support

Ahmes whilst you are away, should that assist Your Eminence."

"That, my dear brother, is why Haremakhet is the royal high priest and not a humble man such as me. What forethought and kindness. I look forward to meeting him in person. Now I must hurry to pack and prepare for my journey. Time is not my friend in this endeavour. Ahmes will make you comfortable and explain the routines and tasks of our small temple. I trust you will follow his guidance. He has considerable expertise in this matter."

"It will be my honour to serve and support a priest of his stature, Your Eminence."

<hr />

Yuya raised a hand to Ahmes and Bebi as his camel laboured up onto four legs. He'd forgone the horse offered by Bebi in favour of the king of the sand. He'd negotiated journeys to and from the temple many times, and he believed he owed his success to always choosing the animal built for the task. Gibil was a wise, albeit somewhat surly desert warrior, and Yuya trusted her to deliver them both safely to Karnak.

He'd decided to travel by the guidance of the stars, when the sun's unforgiving rays were safely tucked away. Although Gibil was well used to the skin-peeling heat of the Southern deserts, he felt it was an act of thoughtful humanity to spare her the endurance test in favour of the brisk evening chills. Both were uncomfortable for him. At times like these, he was thankful his father had passed down the skills of his mariner ways to enable him to plot his journey according to the stars' own maps.

With nothing but the never-ending expanse of sand and

crumbling rock to excite his vision, Yuya lapsed into a deep contemplation about this unusual request from the high priest of Karnak. Yuya had long felt that the rock hand inside the glove of the religious order held back the development of not just the people but, ultimately, the dominion itself. He was excited that Haremakhet appeared to be embracing change.

Yuya was under no illusion that the impact on his little temple would be anything other than minimal but hoped the congress would allow more of Egypt's citizens to enjoy the learnings of the gods. He yearned for all the people of Egypt to bathe in the gods' eternal love. He and Ahmes had long since been offering simple lessons in the ways of Khepri and Montu to any person passing their gate, but few passed. And sadly, even fewer were interested in anything except the blessings of fresh food and water.

Days flowed in a pattern of resting under a fabric shade as Ra blasted burning rays across the sands, then steady progress as the goddess Nut swallowed the sun and heralded the gentle chill of evening and night. Yuya chatted to Gibil as they moved ever closer to their destination.

Slowly, the empty plains of sand became dotted with sparse villages, little more than a couple of mud huts and livestock pens. Yuya found generosity and kindness amongst these most humble of people when he stopped to refresh his water supplies and to say prayers for their good health and future prosperity.

As another morning dawned, he spotted a settlement. It was just a small hut of mud bricks with a fabric awning reaching out to a couple of date palms. A tiny enclosure held a ramshackle collection of livestock. Yuya spotted a swarthy man carrying water buckets towards the parched animals.

The man saw Yuya and put down his load. With a warm smile, he waved him over.

"Welcome, stranger. The gods have blessed us with your presence. Please come inside and rest your weary bones. Yarta, bring beer for our esteemed guest."

The huge man offered his hand up to Yuya, who shook it and tried to climb down from Gibil's solid wooden saddle. His legs trembled as he tried to stand and went into the cramps that had plagued him every morning of the journey. The man hurried to support him.

"You've had a long journey, huh? You would think in this progressive time, we'd have more comfortable means of riding these beasts. I'm Ashrin, by the way. My Yarta's a marvel with a needle. I'll get her to pad this saddle for you whilst you enjoy our hospitality. *Yarta*, hurry with the beer, woman!"

Ashrin half-carried and half-pulled Yuya under a covered lean-to against his hut, which had thick cushions scattered around. He lowered Yuya to the floor.

"Please allow me to assist you, my brother. I have expertise with allaying the pains of the leg. My Yarta is severely tried by the gods—blessings to them—with the affliction."

Yuya, unable to do anything except groan and withhold his screams, nodded his consent. Ashrin pushed Yuya's sand-dyed robes up and manipulated his foot and toes. Yuya screamed and then looked at him in astonishment as the cramp flowed from his leg, leaving him pain-free.

"Your hands must be blessed by Sekhmet herself. How did you do this? I've been wracked with these pains every day of my travels, and they don't ease for hours."

The deep wrinkles around Ashrin's eyes crinkled as he laughed with a boom that ricocheted around the small encampment. "I'm certain our goddess Sekhmet has far worthier people to bless than me. 'Tis but a trick I learnt from Yarta's mother, may the gods bless her departed soul. So, my friend, tell me about yourself. We don't see many travellers in these parts, so the stories you bring are priceless." He turned to look into the hut. "Where is that blasted woman. *Yarta, daughter of Shemak...*"

A tiny woman, not larger than a half-grown child, scuttled out of the hut. Her face was covered with gauze decorated with fine golden chains.

"Husband, stop your shouting. I was addressing the needs of your baby girl. If you want beer, I suggest you pour some from that pitcher on the tray. Welcome, esteemed visitor, to our abode," she said with a deep and gracious bow. "I apologise for the less than refined manners of my husband. What he lacks in brains and manners, he makes up for in looks and ability."

With one last fiery look towards her husband, she swept back into the hut to calm the desperate cries of what sounded like a newborn babe.

Her husband raised his eyes and, with a nervous grimace, said, "What a woman! That's where the gods truly blessed me." He slapped his thigh and burst into booming laughter again.

Yuya nodded as he watched Ashrin pour two deep glasses of beer. Yuya thanked him and drank his in three long gulps.

"Thank you, brother Ashrin, for your hospitality. I'm Yuya, High Priest of Yabaktari, apostle of the gods Khepri and Montu. I'm travelling from my temple to answer the call of our dear Lord Pharaoh and the royal high priest, Haremakhet. They have requested my attendance at a religious congress in the great Karnak temple."

Ashrin leapt to his feet from the cushion he was

sprawled on. "Your Eminence, forgive me. I had no idea," he said, gesticulating with a low bow, his hand on his heart.

Yuya smiled and gestured for Ashrin to be seated again.

"I'm just a weary traveller who couldn't be more grateful for your generous hospitality. Please treat me as such. The title is far grander than I or the position warrants, truly. There is only myself and one other at the temple. It's just a remote dot on the outskirts of the dominion, so I do the work of all positions. Please, my friend, be seated again."

Ashrin sank, somewhat hesitantly, back onto the cushions. "You have given me much joy today, Your Eminence. Please rest here before continuing your journey."

Yuya agreed he would, and the two men resumed their chat, whiling away the hours of the heat of the day.

As they chatted, Yarta and the swaddled baby joined them. After a light lunch, Yarta retrieved her sewing kit and swathes of fabric and sat quietly, listening to their banter whilst she padded the saddle with intricate cushions that fit the hardwood saddle perfectly. Every now and again, she'd interrupt to ask Yuya to try the saddle before continuing with minor adjustments.

As the afternoon sun mellowed, Yuya fell into a deep sleep. He was visited by shadows of the gods, who danced across his mind in a choreographed drama that didn't leave him when he awoke some hours later. Rubbing his eyes, he saw he was alone in the humble shelter lit by burning torches.

In the middle of the shelter sat a saddle such as he'd never witnessed before. Padded to fit the natural lines of his body, the saddle was embroidered with fine stitching. Sewn there were images of Khepri and Montu in fields of flowers and grasses in a shade of green he doubted existed in nature. It was a masterpiece and far too good for a man such as he.

Then he spotted something that brought tears to his eyes. She had paid as much attention to the bottom of the saddle, which sat upon Gibil's back, as to the top on which he sat. It was padded for comfort and embroidered with the delicacies enjoyed by camels.

Such a generous heart belonged to a woman of the gods, he thought.

As he wondered over the skill deployed in the saddle, the dream returned to him. He moved to his travelling pack and withdrew his small altar and statues of his gods. He mapped out a perfect rectangle around the mud shack and set to work blessing the property and its residents. He anointed the door with the holy oils and sprinkled the coloured powders around the doors and windows before lighting the incense and circling the home with its pungent scent.

As he finished, the fabric across the door was pulled aside. Yarta stepped out, looking back to ensure she hadn't disturbed her sleeping family.

"What are you doing, Your Eminence?" she whispered, pointing to the powders and incense.

"The gods have commanded me to grant this abode the Rite of Worship. This is the first time I've been asked to do such a thing. It's extremely rare and a great privilege. It's one you deserve, sister Yarta. Your kindness to Gibil is exceptional, and I thank you sincerely."

Yarta's hands fluttered to her heart as she absorbed his words. "T'was nothing more than normal consideration to all the gods' good creatures," she replied.

Yuya shook his head, "'Tis more precious than all the pharaoh's gold reserves. For as long as your family lives in this spot, you will be guarded by and have the blessings of the gods. Now I must take my leave of you."

Yarta touched his arm reticently. "Please, Your Eminence, allow me to awaken Ashrin. He will be saddened to forgo his farewells."

Smiling at her, Yuya shook his head and patted her hand. Then he moved to saddle up Gibil and repack his meagre provisions upon her wide back. "Please allow him the bliss of deep sleep and give him my sincere and absolute thanks. Both of you have been so kind, and I will not forget that. Now I must take my leave. I can almost smell the Nile's waters, and I don't want to offend our dear Pharaoh or High Priest by tardy timekeeping. Farewell, my dear Yarta, daughter of Shemak. I feel our paths will cross again before our lifes' flames expire."

Gibil lifted him up, grunting curses as she swayed up to her full height. Soon, the veil of darkness hid their progress from Yarta's keen gaze. She looked down and smiled, certain she would see Yuya again. She lifted the curtain, went back inside the hut, and nestled down between her sleeping husband and child.

After another full night in the saddle, Yuya got his first glimpse of the Nile as the sun rose over its glimmering surface. It was wrapped in an emerald cloak of grasses, reeds, and crops. Yuya shoulders dropped, and the stresses of the trip fell away as the early morning breeze brought him the damp, fishy scent of the great river.

He continued on for a while, hoping to find a vessel to transport the two of them the rest of the way to Thebes. After following the river's snaking curves for a couple hours, he found a little bay in the river's side with a small beach and a large pontoon.

With no persuasion, Gibil lowered herself to the ground with a harsh grunt, allowing Yuya to dismount. Yuya unloaded their provisions and removed Gibil's saddle before disrobing and leading his loyal friend into the shallow, lapping waters. Gibil lowered her head and drank as only a camel can, while Yuya let Egypt's life-giver cleanse the dirt of several days from his body and calm his aching muscles.

He floated for a while, enjoying the coolness of the water against his skin as he watched the white egrets search the riverbanks for breakfast. The Nile was a true blessing and Egypt's greatest asset. He knew without it, the people would struggle to eat, and the business of the land would be hindered without its fast and safe passage.

Eventually, he pulled himself from the water's gentle caress and returned to their provisions. He retrieved his oils and incense and redressed in fresh robes. Once he felt he was dressed appropriately, he meditated on the blessings of life before conducting an impromptu and quiet service in honour of Hapi, the god of the Nile. As always, the ritual of religious observance settled him.

They waited out the heat of the day under the shelter of a nearby palm tree. Gibil nibbled on dried dates around its base, flapping her tail at the endless parade of flies surrounding them. As the day cooled and the sun dropped ever lower, a large vessel docked at the pontoon.

The boat's deck was empty, except for a couple of large baskets of ducks at the front. The captain was a small but muscle-bound man whose skin had been cured a deep ebony by years of exposure to the harsh Egyptian sun. He was sucking on a sugar cane stem as he secured the boat to the pontoon.

"Good evening, Captain. How fortuitous to find you

docking here. I'm Yuya, High Priest of Yabaktari, apostle of the gods Khepri and Montu. Where are you heading?"

Turning at Yuya's words, the captain studied him with shrewd eyes. "I don't offer charity to no religious types. Your sort's never done me any favours, so I don't much see why I should offer you any." He spat out a wad of the sugar's outer skin and resumed gnawing at the cane.

"My good man, I wouldn't expect free passage. I have payment."

The captain studied him, looking him up and down. "Show me your payment, and we can talk."

Yuya bowed his head, acknowledging the man's request. He opened a bag to reveal some turquoise donated to the coffers of Yabaktari by one of the caravan traders that infrequently stopped for blessings and respite from the desert sun. The captain looked down into the purse at the precious stone, and his eyes gleamed.

"So, where is it you wish to travel to, Your Eminence? It would be my honour to carry you on my humble vessel. Anything for the gods, you understand. I'm docked here to pick up some grain destined for the pharaoh's tithe in Thebes."

Yuya smiled at this immediate turn of face in the presence of turquoise and realised that the god this man worshipped was gold. "I'm delighted to hear that for I am travelling to the same destination. I didn't catch your name, my friend."

"Qrata's the name. I'm the owner of this barge and one other too. She's being run by staff. Normally, you understand, I wouldn't be working this one. I have people to do that, but sometimes it pays to keep a working eye on your business. You can be robbed blind otherwise."

Yuya looked at his sun-scorched skin and smiled wryly.

"Indeed. It makes good sense, Captain Qrata. I commend you for staying in touch with the working man."

The two men loaded Gibil onto the barge and secured Yuya's possessions whilst they waited for the grain delivery. Finally, a long chain of water buffalo plodded towards them in a dust cloud, each buffalo loaded with two panniers of grain.

Yuya studied the exchange between the humble farmer and the shrewd captain and soon realised the farmer was hopelessly outwitted by Qrata, who was charging far more than was respectable for the tithe's passage.

"My dear captain, I don't think you understood me. I'm paying for the hire of the entire barge. I'm happy to allow this hard-working farmer's tithe to travel as well without sharing the costs." He turned back to the farmer. "If that's okay with you, sir?"

Qrata ground his teeth but could say nothing.

The farmer raised objections, which Yuya soon overcame, and the three men worked to load the barge with the grain parcels.

"Thank you for your kindness, sir. I will use this windfall to invest in more seeds to extend my crops. I want my young son to have an education, to be more than me. His mother—gods bless her soul—was such a smart woman, and he takes that from her. It would've pleased her to see her son raised higher than our humble existence."

Yuya took the farmer's hand. "'Tis nothing, my good man. Allow me a moment to ask the gods to support you in your noble efforts."

After a short prayer of blessings to both Khepri and Montu, Qrata and Yuya took their leave of the farmer and eased the barge into the Nile.

"You wasted your blessing there, Your Eminence.

Nothing will come of that fool and his son. The man can't see his way around a barter. He'll never afford an education for his boy. The gods bless those who bless themselves."

"We'll see, my friend," Yuya said with a smile. "The gods rarely let me down, but we'll see."

With the river's fast flow and strong winds in their sails, the barge cut through the Nile, eating the distance far quicker than Gibil's four legs would have done. Despite his protestations to the contrary, Qrata's daily knowledge of the river's quirks held them in good stead, allowing them to travel in low light when many other boats retired. They made good time, with Yuya gritting his teeth and smiling through Qrata's endless stories of his financial conquests.

Yuya was stood in the bow of the barge, stroking the rope like muscles of Gibil's neck, when he spotted Thebes in the distance. The mighty temple of Karnak glowed like a gold beacon. It towered over the mud dwellings that cowered at its feet. Just moments later, they docked at the vast pontoons that serviced the capital's needs.

Yuya joined the procession of priests who'd travelled from across the pharaoh's wide lands by boat, donkey, or camel. Some, from the wealthier temples, came by horse. As he guided Gibil towards the temple, he chatted to them. All had endured difficult journeys, with the heat oppressive, the terrain difficult, and the distance long. Many of the priests had conducted services in the villages they travelled through, spreading the word of the gods' good graces.

"Have you heard the purpose of this congress?" one elderly priest asked from his perch on Gibil's back, having accepted Yuya's earlier offer of passage.

"Only the same as you, I imagine. I've spoken to a few of our brethren, and we all seem to have received an identical message. It's intriguing, is it not? I do hope it's the beginning of a more open and inclusive attitude."

"Hmph. Can't see what's wrong with what we've been doing since the gods gifted us with the knowledge of their being. Change rarely improves anything in my experience. The masses are too stupid and too ill-informed to deserve or be able to comprehend such breadth of philosophy as our gods have blessed us with."

Yuya sighed before turning to the old man and smiling with a bow. "Your experience outweighs mine considerably, Your Eminence." He changed the man's focus by pointing out some fine fabrics and spices on the stalls that lined their route. They continued the rest of their journey in companionable chatter.

The procession made their way to the vast tent erected outside of the temple's walls. It was clear whoever had organised the event was keen to make a statement. Yuya looked around at the extravagant show of wealth and power. He was saddened that the high priest had poured such huge resources into the event and suspected the changes he hoped for were unlikely, based on this show.

He jumped as a blast from a horn announced their arrival. They were heralded with pipes and drums and guided to the crimson tent. It was draped with banners of the pharaoh's cartouche embroidered in gold threads. The canopy was topped with finials of the great gods.

As Yuya entered the tent, a slight breeze fluttered over his brow, cooling the sweat beads and swirling the curling trails of incense. He saw the slaves pumping a device that moved the weaved palm frond fans which hung above their heads. Carpets of red, turquoise, and green covered the floor, and plush cushions were scattered around tables covered with juices and light refreshments for the weary travellers. He took a cooled cloth scented with rose water from a young female slave and wiped his face and hands. With flutes playing gentle, hypnotic tunes, he and his fellow priests introduced themselves.

Yuya and the rest of the priests waited in the tent until the sun dipped on the horizon. They discussed their temples, sharing stories of the gods' good graces and their own daily rituals. Yuya found the chatter insightful, showing the clear divide between the progressive priests and the more traditional faction. He was proud that arguments were averted as his brethren adopted a policy of tolerance over conviction.

As the sun descended for its evening's sleep, large metal braziers of logs and perfumed barks were lit outside the tent, leading up to the entrance of the temple. The flames, playing in the breeze from the Nile, sent shadows leaping across the facade. The tent emptied as the priests loitered outside, eager to see what would follow.

A massed band of musicians, so large that they covered most of the temple's outer courtyard, heralded the arrival of a rotund man at the temple's entrance. He was lit by torch bearers and slaves bearing mirrors, which they angled to light his features.

"Welcome, my brothers." His voice boomed across the courtyard, clear to every member of the amassed orders of Khepri, Sobek, and Bastet. "I am Pabasa, the deputy high priest of Karnak. I welcome you to this first religious congress held under the auspices of our great and most beloved Pharaoh. May the gods bestow their blessings on you."

He waited as the priests stamped their approval. The

sound of the massed feet echoed around the temple grounds.

"You have all travelled far and suffered much to attend this event, so tonight, let's celebrate your safe arrival and enjoy the pharaoh's bounty. Welcome to the holy temple of Karnak. Come, follow me."

Dancers and acrobats moved with them, swaying to the music and guiding them across the carpet of herbs laid across the path and into the temple.

The temple was lit with lanterns and large torches that created pools of light at the base of the towering columns. The metal disk mirrors attached to the walls bounced the meagre glow around the chamber. Pabasa, in his finest robes, greeted each priest at the door leading to the holy lake, on which floated pontoons with blazing braziers that reflected in the pool's mirror-like surface. It was truly a sight to behold and alien to most of the priests who came from relatively poor temples.

Yuya's hopes dipped further.

THE SELECTION

As the attendees rolled into Thebes, Pabasa held nightly banquets to welcome the new arrivals. Both Kiya and Haremakhet avoided these rituals, preferring to meet the candidates when they'd all arrived and the event convened.

Haremakhet felt the events were ostentatious but didn't demure or voice his concerns to ensure he maintained his deputy's support and enthusiasm for the congress. Pabasa revelled in the atmosphere and the prestige the event bestowed upon him. As the days passed, he glided around the temple, riding his ego.

"Have you noticed Pabasa's demeanour since the priests started arriving?" Haremakhet asked Kiya one hot afternoon whilst they planned the assessment criteria.

Kiya raised her eyes from her scrying mirror, the blue brighter than normal and shining with mirth. She grinned at Haremakhet and raised her eyebrows. "I think you've unleashed a monster within him," she laughed. "I saw him yesterday giving a sermon to some older priests about the blessings of death. They were squirming at his descriptions. I think it's a prospect rather closer to them than they'd like."

Haremakhet rubbed his neck and sighed. "A little power can pollute the best of men. Pabasa has always been power-hungry, yet can lack the piety to achieve it through his own devotions and hard work. I fear he will be unbearable for a while."

Kiya leaned across and patted his hand. "Don't worry. He's a good man at heart. He will return to his less-inflated self when the congress is over."

"Have you seen that?" Haremakhet asked.

"No, just my intuition speaking," Kiya said as a frown darkened her brow. "I still haven't had a new vision. All I see is the downfall of our empire. The temples being buried under the desert sands until just the roofs peek out. Our pharaohs' bodies being desecrated, removed from their tombs and displayed for people's pleasure. Our great discoveries and learnings lost, and our people returned to a time of ignorance. It disturbs me so much to see our destruction played out repeatedly."

She shook her head, looking down to study the stitching of her robe. "It's only knowing we are helping to restore the balance that makes it endurable." Sighing, she moved to the fountain and cupped her hand to form a vessel for the water. She splashed some of the cool water onto her face.

"You've never told me what you see of the House of Scarabs," Haremakhet said, following her example and cooling his brow with the fountain's water.

Kiya's eyes dilated, and she looked into the distance. It was not a distance that Haremakhet could see but one showing her far into the future.

"I see the three gods, in their spirit form, embedded within the very being of three people. A woman of courage and fragility, with hair of fire and a temper to match. A man of purpose and vigour, a protector in the full flush of manhood, with skin dark like the shell of a nut. An old man of learning and wisdom, with a mind as strong as our mighty Aswan granite. By dying, they will be raised again and form an impenetrable bond that opens the gods' powers and raises our long-dead pharaohs. They will suffer much during their initiation, but the gods will grant them immunity from death until they decide to pass the gift onto their children or choose to carry it forever. It's a heavy burden they will carry for our benefit."

Kiya shook her head and focused her eyes on Haremakhet.

"Your own gift comes with a heavy burden, my dear," Haremakhet murmured as he pondered all she'd told him. "I hope they can one day forgive us the burden we'll place upon them."

Kiya disappeared into another trance. Haremakhet watched her expressions flicker from surprise to fear until her face settled into stoic determination. As she turned to him, her eyes changed to emerald green with crescents of the deepest amber.

A rich voice different to Kiya's sweet tone said, "They will, our son, for Kiya will guide them towards their destiny. Kiya will become the House of Scarabs' seer."

Kiya's eyes returned to their beautiful blue and stared at Haremakhet. "It seems my duties will last beyond this life and this body. I fear we have much more to plan than I'd envisaged."

Haremakhet nodded.

Nimlot woke from the dream screaming, his bed shirt clinging to his damp body. He glanced around the tent, checking he hadn't disturbed his brethren. Sitting up, he swept his trembling hand over his head and threw his feet onto the compacted earth floor. Moving silently, he dressed and left the tent, needing solitude to calm his feverish mind.

The chill of predawn hugged the temple complex as he followed the moon's rays towards the sacred lake. The calm waters drew him forward. Never in his twenty summers of religious observation had he felt so uncertain and tortured.

Ever since his father had died, leaving him the sole provider for a house of six women, Nimlot had followed a path of serene certainty. He'd felt the lure of the gods deep in his soul, calling him to serve them. Reassuring him that in doing so, his family would prosper, and they had.

He'd married four of his five sisters to fine and well-established men, and the fifth had followed him into the service of the gods. His mother had a secure income from his own purse. Whilst he missed his father, he felt satisfied that if he were to meet him again, he could do so proudly.

The dreams had changed everything. They'd started six full moons ago. The themes varied little, and it was the ceaseless repetition that was wearing him down like a fine drop of water on stone. Death, annihilation, and rebirth.

Sometimes he saw the people of the dominion throwing the gods into a fire and laughing as they burned. He and two others would run forward and throw themselves onto the fire, suffocating the flames. The three would take the burnt husks of the gods and eat their bodies, consuming them until nothing remained.

The seasons ticked by in seconds until they were fragile old men. From their bodies burst babies, who morphed into old men from which more babies burst. Generation after generation until, in an act of barbaric cannibalism, a far-removed generation consumed each other. The babies lay in a circle. Each took the feet of the baby in front into their mouths, then started chewing up the body until just three heads remained. As the heads consumed each other, they blinked out of existence. All that remained were the tiny blue bodies of the gods Khepri, Bastet, and his own dear Sobek.

Nimlot reflected on the horror of the dream. Although far less gruesome, there was one dream that haunted him. He'd watch, a frozen spectator, as each of the gods filed into their temples across the dominion. The gods ambled around the temples dedicated to them, touching statues erected to celebrate their greatness, brushing aside a stray cobweb or dust. Slowly, as if capturing memories, they moved toward the holy of holies and lay down to sleep, covering themselves with the finest of gauze sheets.

The sun rose and set. Dust drifted down, resting on the sheets. Sand piled up around them. Time passed, season after season flowing by. The temples fell into disrepair, the gods buried under mounds of desert sand. Alone they slept. No one visited. No one worshipped. They were forgotten to time.

Then, one by one, people returned and cleared the temples. More and more came, invading the sacred ground of the holy of holies. They passed around and over the gods unseeing, as if the gods were not there or did not exist. It was from this dream that Nimlot most often woke screaming.

He watched the gentle ripples of the water playing under the moon's soft caress. What could it mean? How could he prevent it happening? These were the questions plaguing him. He'd prayed for guidance, but so far, the gods hadn't answered him. He'd doubled, then trebled his devotionals, hoping that greater religious observations may give him guidance. Doubts grew. He felt himself questioning how the great gods could allow such a cataclysmic event to occur. They wouldn't, of course.

Nimlot's hands shook as he faced his greatest fear. Was he falling prey to the illness that had taken his father? Those last months of his father's life were ingrained in his memory. The delusions, the anger that would spike from nowhere. His father had studied the law and been one of the pharaoh's great advisors until his judgement became so impaired, he'd wrongly prosecuted a young boy to death. Disgraced, the family had left Thebes and returned to their mother's country home, shielding the once-great man as his mind crumbled into a land far away from sanity. His death had been a release for them all.

Nimlot took a steadying breath and revisited his actions of the previous day, checking he'd behaved rationally. The fear that he wouldn't recognise irrational behaviour surfaced again, as it did every night. He would not jeopardise his family's good name. Should he spot abnormal behaviour, he'd committed to take his own life and face the gods' retribution to preserve his mother and sister's good name. He would not allow them to be disgraced again.

His muscles had cramped, so he eased himself up and set off across the complex, determined to see the dawn in with a series of devotionals. Come what may, he'd find a solution and protect both his gods and his family.

The day of the congress's opening dawned bright, with breezes that lifted the oppressive heat of the previous weeks. All the attendants took this to be a blessing of the event by the gods.

Pabasa had organised the dismantling of the welcome tent overnight, and it was now re-erected within the walls of the temple.

The priests enjoyed a breakfast of bread soaked in cream and honey before being guided to the tent.

"Do you suppose that buffoon will give another speech on our luck to be welcomed into his 'most holy of temples'?" asked a priest Yuya had come to know rather well.

"Nimlot, be kind, my friend. He's just proud of his temple and keen to share that joy with us. Aren't we all proud of our temples?"

Nimlot studied Yuya silently before answering. "Yes, brother, but not to the detriment or belittling of others."

Yuya inclined his head in a nod. "True. Let's pray for the return of his humility."

"Pay no attention to me, my friend. I fear lack of sleep is adding a degree of bitterness to my tongue. I'm sure he's a good man."

"I'd have thought the pharaoh's fine beer would have been a great sleep aid. You surely drank enough of it last night. I slept the sleep of an innocent babe," Yuya replied with a grin.

"Sadly not, but it did enhance my nightmares. No matter. Shall we go?"

Pabasa had organised for a stage to be erected at the far end of the tent, and it was onto this that Haremakhet and Kiya climbed. They stopped behind the curtain as Pabasa gave his opening speech. He'd orchestrated the proceedings in fine detail and had informed them of the cue for the curtains to open and reveal them.

"This feels ridiculous. I'm a man of the gods, not a jester or stage actor. It's undignified," Haremakhet grumbled under his breath.

"At least you put your foot down when it came to his costume ideas. Although, I'd have loved to see you in the mask of Osiris," Kiya giggled.

Haremakhet shook his head and laughed. "You may laugh, but he had the mask of Isis and sheer gold robes for you."

Kiya shuddered. "That wasn't ever going to happen." She pulled back the curtains a crack to peer at the priests facing the stage. Some at the back were snoozing through Pabasa's big speech. "Poor souls are being bored into submission," she whispered. "I keep expecting to see a large pointer above the head of our candidates but so far, nothing. All I see are a bunch of hot and restless priests."

They stopped and listened to Pabasa's speech.

"The time comes when the great and the wise must share some of their experience with the lesser mortals, those still entrenched in the darkness of ignorance and of poverty. It is for that reason we've brought you to the glorious and most holy temple of Karnak, to share our wisdom and allow you to bathe in the glory of our knowledge. Today, I will introduce you to the two most important religious and state leaders. It's vital you address them with respect and decorum. Don't feel you are amongst your brothers of faith. No! For you will be in the presence of your superiors, and..."

"In all the gods' glorious names! Enough is enough. I think I've given Pabasa enough headroom," Haremakhet said, striding through the curtains and onto the stage. Kiya hurried in his wake.

With huge belly laughs, Haremakhet strode up to his deputy and wrapped him in a crushing embrace. "Pabasa, your comedy knows no boundaries," he said, turning to Kiya. "He's jesting again, Your Omniscience. Come, everyone. Show your appreciation for Pabasa's comedic turn. He knows how to start the day with laughter. We should all follow his guidance and take life and ourselves less seriously."

Pabasa turned back to the audience with a mottled red face to accept the pounding stamps of their appreciation. "I haven't finished my welcome speech," he hissed out the side of his mouth at Haremakhet whilst trying to look pleased with the state of affairs.

"Yes, Pabasa, you have," Haremakhet said, guiding him off the stage.

"My brothers, it warms my heart to see so many learned and pious men here in our humble temple. You have honoured us with your presence. I, like you, am a High Priest, a man of the gods. We are equal under the gods' eyes, merely mortals trying to please our beloved gods, one and all. I am Haremakhet. You've already met my dear brother, Pabasa, and this gentle lady is Kiya, our pharaoh's High Seer. Please address us by our given names as Pabasa so eloquently showed there is no place for pomposity at this congress."

Yuya turned to Nimlot with raised eyebrows and whispered, "Things are looking up, my friend."

From the stage, Kiya's voice hypnotised the men as she outlined the plans for the three days.

"Thank you, Haremakhet. My dear friends, you may have wondered why you have been called here under the auspices of the pharaoh. I'm afraid I am responsible for your trying journeys. The gods blessed me with a vision of the three houses of Sobek, Bastet, and Khepri holding a religious congress here in Karnak. This congress will result in much progress for our beloved dominion and our people. Although I was shown the barest glimpse of the event, I know its outcome will preserve our faith and our ways long into the future."

She stopped and looked at the men with an ethereal smile.

"The days will pass as follows. We will divide into the houses. Pabasa will explore the current habits and practises of each temple within the house and facilitate learnings we can take from each other. Haremakhet will oversee a discussion on new ideas and approaches we can implement for the improvement of our faith and our people. I will explore the issues that require the gods' intervention or wisdoms, and I'll attempt to use my powers of vision to answer some of those concerns." She smiled, making eye contact with everyone in the tent. "We will have open minds, open hearts, and accepting souls so that the gods can guide us as we explore these new paths."

Yuya beamed at Nimlot. "It seems the gods have already listened to our prayers. This may prove to be life-changing."

Nimlot stroked his finely trimmed beard. "We can hope, Yuya. We can hope."

As the sun set over the Nile, Kiya called a halt to the day's proceedings. She had a brief discussion with her group's scribe to ensure he'd captured all the pertinent points before picking up her scrying mirror and turning to leave the fountain courtyard. Smiling politely at all the lingering participants, she stopped to talk as some asked her to repeat finer points of her visions.

She'd been dreading her part in the congress, sure her visions would continue to fail her. Instead, her inner eye opened and flooded her with images and scenes. The visions came so quickly, she almost couldn't explain them before another started.

A muscular, tall man with a finely manicured beard lingered on the edge of the group. She noticed his reticence to talk in front of the remaining priests, so she answered their questions until they were the only two remaining.

"Your Omniscience," he said with a bow and hand over his heart.

"Kiya, please," she answered with a smile.

"I am Nimlot of Kom Ombo, and I wondered if I may talk privately with you?"

"Well, we can try. There's precious little privacy around this temple right now. Why don't we walk whilst we chat?"

She looked up into his eyes and jumped back. Nimlot looked at her quizzically, his deep brown eyes changing to emerald green framed with amber crescents.

"I'm sorry. I had a stutter in my vision—nothing to worry about. It happens all the time," she said. "Let's walk." She reached across and linked her arm in his.

As soon as they touched, she saw Sobek, the crocodile god, appear from a glowing orb of blue energy. It swirled and twisted as he glided towards them, throwing out wispy strands of energy. His image solidified as it neared them, still glowing with the strange blue energy but clearer to her eye. He towered two heads above both Kiya and Nimlot. From the neck down, he had the form of a man with perfect musculature and skin that glowed. Kiya found herself terrified to look up at his huge reptilian head, his eyes studying her above rows of sharp ivory teeth.

Sobek touched Nimlot, and everything froze. Not a bird sang or a leaf fluttered. Even the clouds had stopped moving. The world was immobile, and the only two conscious beings were Sobek and Kiya. She looked around, studying this strange phenomenon.

"Do not be frightened, my daughter. I bear you no harm. Quite the contrary." Sobek spoke into Kiya's mind. His voice was perfectly melodious, yet not a sound passed his lips. "We have been watching you for some time, testing you to see if you are the one with the fortitude for our task. We're pleased with you, daughter. You have handled yourself with decorum and character. Your strength and determination will leave you in good stead in the years and centuries to come."

Kiya's gaze jumped up to his eyes. "Centuries? But I am just a mortal. My lifetime is short."

"Your lifetime knows no bounds. It will not be measured by the current vessel's survival, for it's your soul that will serve us. You will be our voice in this mortal realm. You will see with our eyes and guide our mortal carriers."

Sobek turned and surveyed Nimlot, studying him like the chariot drivers did their prize stallions. He walked around Nimlot, studying him from every angle before gliding his hand into Nimlot's chest and cupping his heart.

"This man will be the founder of the House of Sobek. He and his descendants will fight to protect and support the other two houses. Nimlot will be the protector, the guardian. He will carry me."

Sobek faded, taking his ephemeral form again.

"My God Sobek, how will I persuade him to undertake this role?" Kiya asked.

"He has seen many things that will persuade him this is his destiny. None of us can escape our destiny, my sweet one, not even us gods. Farewell, Kiya, High Seer of Karnak and overseer of the gods of Sobek, Bastet, and Khepri."

The orb extended its arms to embrace and enfold Sobek, whose energy merged with the sphere and disappeared. The world stumbled forward again.

Nimlot caught Kiya's arm as she stumbled, "Are you all right?"

"'Tis nothing. I felt a little faint. Sorry, what where you saying?" Kiya replied smoothly, long used to covering her lapses in concentration when visions took her elsewhere.

She studied this man chosen by the gods to start a mission that would burden his family for generations. He seemed earnest and pious, which counted for much in Kiya's mind. Too many of the people that surrounded the pharaoh were men of greed. They were thirsty for power, and yet, no matter how much they gained, it never quenched them. Few of the priests had the piety and character of Haremakhet, but this man seemed close.

"What concerns you, Nimlot, that you seek council from the high seer? It is the high seer you seek now, rather than a humble slave woman's opinion, is that not so?"

Nimlot met her steady gaze. "I seek your council, all the shades that make you Kiya the woman and the High Seer."

He glanced down at his hands, walking silently for a few paces. Kiya let him gather his thoughts in silence.

"Kiya, is it possible for a person without the gift of the sight to have visions of the future?" Without letting her answer, he continued, "I've heard of maladies that can create mental confusion, but they present themselves continuously. I've seen such things, I fear it can only be an illness of the mind, and yet, deep down, I feel the truth of the vision. I'm confused—may the gods bear witness against me—and conflicted. If what I see is true, I must bear news to the high priest of Karnak and the pharaoh, but if it's a malady, they will remove me from my position. I support my mother and sisters. I can't afford to lose that." He kicked the stones at his feet and held his head in both hands. "What am I to do?"

Kiya studied him, waiting for him to raise his head and look at her. In a bid to provide reassurance, she smiled gently at him. "I have the answer to your dilemma, but now is not the time for its telling. Be patient, my dear man, and be reassured that you have no malady. The gods can open channels to anyone, even those without the gift of the sight. All will make sense soon. For now, share these visions with me and no one else. That is of vital importance. Now tell Kiya..."

The next morning, over breakfast, there was a buzz of excitement that had been missing in the previous days. Only a few naysayers were grumbling about tradition, but even they'd been allayed by the careful weaving of tradition and change that Haremakhet and Kiya had created in the congress's agenda.

Yuya and Nimlot had become fast friends, sharing much of the same philosophy about their beliefs. They both hoped to see the elitist barriers of the religious practises being lowered to allow the humble subjects of the pharaoh greater access to the temples and spiritual learnings.

"How went yesterday, my friend?" asked Yuya whilst chewing a mouthful of bread. "You were with Kiya, were you not?"

Dipping his own bread in honey, Nimlot nodded. "She was amazing. I'd heard rumours she is the most powerful high seer to have ever served a pharaoh, and now I believe that to be more than an idle rumour. She had answers to every query my brothers raised. Her answers were considered and often seemed contrary to public opinion, yet not one of my fellow priests questioned her responses. I think we will all return to our temples far richer for this experience, armed with wisdom and enthusiasm. How went your day?"

"Not as inspirational as yours, I fear, but productive nevertheless. It worried me we'd have more of Pabasa's puffery, but he adjudicated the meeting well, and I will take many ideas back to Yabaktari. It's amazing the ingenuity of the human mind, don't you think?"

Nimlot nodded as he took a long draft of the spiced warm milk. Wiping his mouth, he picked at some grapes. "Indeed, it is. Praise be to the gods for our blessings."

Yuya joined him in his thanks before rising from the bench. "Let us hope today is equally productive." He took his leave, keen to have some moments of religious introspection before the day's proceedings began.

Yuya found a quiet place near one corner of the sacred lake. Ants scurried and crickets jumped around him. He sat cross-legged upon the ground, watching the tiny creatures hurrying about their daily routines. He often took comfort in knowing the gods came in many forms, from the smallest of insects to the largest of predators.

As he watched, a scarab beetle marched towards him, undaunted at the disparate size difference between them. The scarab rose onto its back legs as if gesturing for a fight.

"Ah, my dear God Khepri, good morning to you." Yuya

bowed from the waist and placed his hand over his heart in the traditional pose of deference.

"You've found a benefactor, I see." Yuya looked over his shoulder to see Kiya walking towards him. She bent low, her white robe dusting the ground as she offered her hand to the beetle. The little fellow stopped his gesturing and lifted into the air to land in her palm. "They're beautiful creatures, don't you think?"

"I do, but as an apostle of Khepri, I'm bound to."

"And yet, I've seen only you bow to the creature in deference to the god. It's telling. Would you care to accompany me and my little friend here on our walk, Yuya?"

He looked up into her blazing emerald eyes, noticing the flaming amber crescents. "You know my name?"

"I know much about you." She smiled, gesturing to her other hand. "He's told me your story. Paying for the buffalo's passage was a most generous gesture."

Yuya jumped, shocked that she could know such a minor detail. He stood up and brushed the dust from his robe, steadying his nerves before once again meeting her thoughtful gaze. She smiled at him, gesturing towards a path that led away from the lake.

"As you found my favourite spot already, I'll share another with you. Follow me."

Kiya chatted idly as they walked, asking him questions about Yabaktari and Ahmes before leading him to a tiny chapel far from the main complex. She turned to him, offering her free hand. As they touched, the scarab rattled its wings together, letting out a haunting tune.

Blue wisps of moving light circled it, swirling ever faster and growing with every rotation. The scarab raised up into the air and moved a couple of paces away, a stationary point in a whirlpool of energy. It locked Yuya solid. Quite unable to move, he felt Kiya stroke his hand, offering comfort in this moment of wonder. As he watched, the scarab evaporated into the energy and emerged as a man with the head of Khepri.

Kiya swept into an elegant bow, her hand across her heart. "My God Khepri, you honour us with your presence."

Khepri nodded at her and turned to face Yuya. He tilted his head.

Kiya touched Yuya's arm. "He wishes to talk to you via me. He wants to know if you will converse with him."

Yuya felt his muscles relax and movement return. "It would be an honour beyond anything I deserve," he answered.

A voice of authority and masculine weight came from Kiya's mouth. "Please anoint this temple with a prayer for me, and we shall shelter within its shade."

Yuya turned to him. "I will hurry back for my oils and powders."

"My son, you need them not. Your love, belief, and conviction hold greater significance than those trifles. Just speak the words of the prayer from your heart."

Yuya looked at the god, ensuring he'd heard him correctly. Khepri nodded his head slowly. Yuya shrugged and chanted the age-old prayer of thanks and benediction. It felt odd to go against his learnings, but who better to advise him than the god to which he prayed?

As soon as the prayers were completed, Khepri gestured for Kiya and Yuya to precede him into the small chapel. It was an old building and by far the smallest of Karnak's varied offerings. Infrequently used, its interior hadn't been illuminated with candles, so they walked into blackness. Khepri followed them, and with a twirl of his hand, the blue sphere filled the door, sealing them into the temple and others out.

The eerie blue glow lit the temple, showing the tired interior. Sand drifted across the floor in piles, and spiders had decorated the room with large, complex webs. A dove was nesting in a small alcove. She cooed to welcome them and flew up and around Khepri before settling on his raised hand. He stroked her, and she moved her head to meet his attentions in a state of bliss.

"They are innocent souls, taking nothing more than they need, harming nothing in their struggle for existence. Humans could learn much from them. Come, little lady. Attend to your babies." Kiya spoke Khepri's words as he took the dove to her nest and settled her back amongst her chicks.

Yuya watched as Khepri approached Kiya and appeared to be talking silently to her. She nodded and smiled at him before they both turned back to face Yuya.

"Our God Khepri has asked if he may use my body to communicate with you. Do you concur?"

Yuya nodded slowly. Khepri moved toward Kiya before dissolving into raw, blue, pulsing energy that swirled around Kiya, wrapping her in the ephemeral form of Khepri. It reminded him of the jellyfish he'd seen in his youth. It had eaten a small fish, and he'd seen both the form of the jellyfish and the form of its food through its transparent body.

"I've been searching for some time for an apostle to help me with a task of such magnitude, it could very well define the future of all Egypt and even my reign as a god. We will face troubled times, my son, times when our faith will be lost, forgotten, and buried under the sands of time. We'll be relegated to stories told to children, just a historical by-line.

Our ways, our knowledge, our culture, and our power of resurrection will all disappear and be lost to human memory. I need someone to carry the seed of our faith and our ability through time to enable us to, one day, reassert ourselves and regain our place in the world.

"I have decided that person should be you. What I ask of you isn't an easy path to follow. It's neither safe nor comfortable. You will be committing yourself and your descendants to a burden that you will carry until the end of time. For that reason, I request your support, rather than demand it. Only two other people know of this mission: Kiya and Haremakhet. In them you can trust. If you agree to carry the seed of Khepri, you will join two others who will carry Bastet and Sobek.

"Kiya grows weary. I will leave you to ponder on my words before you give your decision to Kiya. Should you decline, I will naturally be disappointed, but no harm will come to you. I value your service and respect your integrity. Think on it, my son. Should you have questions, put them to Kiya. I needn't tell you the importance of secrecy. Please do not talk of this outside the circle of current knowledge."

Khepri studied Yuya's wide-eyed shock, tipping his head to one side before nodding and waving farewell. With that, his energy dispersed, returning to the swirling mass in the doorway. It contracted, shrinking ever smaller until just a tiny blue scarab remained on the floor. It raised up on its rear legs and flew away, leaving Kiya and Yuya alone in the dark chapel.

"Did you hear what he said?" Yuya asked immediately. Kiya nodded thoughtfully before crossing to his side, looping her arm through his and leading them both out into the sun.

"These are difficult times, my friend. Think hard on his

words, and don't take the decision lightly."

"Why me? I don't understand. It's too vast a job, too important a job for a lesser priest such as me. But then who am I to question the will of my god?"

"Khepri wouldn't have chosen you if he didn't believe you encapsulated all the characteristics he's looking for. Don't doubt yourself, Your Eminence."

Kiya smiled silently as Yuya contemplated all he had heard.

"I doubt his judgement not Kiya. Indeed this is a great blessing, but I fear I may not have the strength to carry the burden of it. I must consider this carefully, for I'm not committing myself only. I'm impacting the destiny of all my descendants. I know I will happily die in the service of my gods, but do I have the right to make that decision for my children and their children down through time?"

They walked back in companionable silence to the courtyard of fountains to join the massed ranks Khepri's High Priests.

Haremakhet paced the tight constraints of his humble quarters, his toes puffing up the dust like sand from the floor. He'd had the same room in the priest's quarters since he was an initiate, never taking the prestigious dwellings his rising rank proffered. Instead, Pabasa enjoyed the high priest's villa, more than happy to benefit from what he considered Haremakhet's peculiar principles.

The room was plainly furnished, with just a simple cot, wooden chair, and a small coffer for clothes and personal possessions. There was an alcove adorned with statues of some gods that Haremakhet used as an altar to focus his prayers each night before he slept. Otherwise, the room was bare of any comforts or decoration. Normally, it brought Haremakhet a tranquillity he lacked in his daily life, but today was not such a day.

He'd just received a message from the pharaoh, announcing his plans to travel upriver for the day. That in itself was not unusual or troubling, but his request for Kiya to accompany him threw their carefully planned congress into utter disarray. The pharaoh had offered to replace Kiya with another of the palace's lesser seers, but without Kiya meeting the candidates for the House of Bastet, Haremakhet feared their plan was doomed to failure.

He'd been struggling to think of a way to change the pharaoh's plans but with little success. What the pharaoh wanted, he always got, as sure as the sun rose over the Nile each morning. They were so close to delivering the three candidates. Surely, the gods wouldn't abandon them now. He turned to the altar and started his morning rituals, hoping the gods would answer him.

As he threw the bowl of washing water on the roots of the abundant flowering vine that ambled up his outer wall, he felt no closer to a solution. He shrugged into his outer robe, took one deep breath, and stepped outside to attempt to correct the day's trajectory.

He'd sent a messenger to the palace seer, asking for her to meet him in the fountain courtyard. She was new to the role, and he hadn't yet met her. As he approached the courtyard, he racked his brain for a solution that would allow the selection to go ahead. Tomorrow, the gathered priests would leave, and the congress would be over. Unless the selection was made today, all hope of creating the House of Scarabs would dwindle. The gods remained resolutely silent, providing no guidance.

It felt odd to Haremakhet to see another seer in the place he so strongly associated with Kiya. The girl looked no more than ten and six years old, barely old enough to have experienced life, let alone hold the future of Egypt in her delicate hands. Unlike Kiya, she covered her face with a swathe of sheer fabric decorated with golden chains and beads. Warm ebony eyes looked up at him through outlined eyelashes. There was no doubt she was a native of the dominion. Her olive skin and black hair hinted her lineage was from the Upper Lands.

She bowed low, with her hand placed devoutly across her heart. *Oh, for the flexibility of youth,* Haremakhet thought as she effortlessly rose up to her full height, one that brought the top of her head to Haremakhet's upper arm. *I pray the gods support your efforts on this day, my dear girl,* he thought before acknowledging her with a bow of his own.

"Your Eminence, it's a privilege beyond my ability to express to be graced with the opportunity to meet you today. I am honoured to serve you and your peers at this great congress."

Haremakhet smiled gently at her and gave her hand a pat. "Thank you for your kind words, my dear. I suggest you wait until the end of the day before you make a judgement on the greatness of the congress."

She shuffled and blushed, looking down. "I'm sorry. I didn't mean to make assumptions. It's just everyone in the palace and temple are talking about the event, and without exception, I've heard positive things. I will reserve judgement and make my decision as should a seer of my position. I apologise."

"My dear, it is I who should apologise for making you uncomfortable. I was but joking with you. I'm ashamed to have brought a blush to your cheek. Pray tell, your name?"

Her soft eyes raised hesitantly to meet his, and a smile peeked out, creating huge dimples in her cheeks. "I am Laqma."

"Well, Laqma, come. We have much to discuss. Kiya was running an entire branch of the congress by herself, and I must brief you on the duties you will bear today. After that, would you care to accompany me to breakfast? I find the gods communicate better when I've a full stomach, don't you?"

She glanced up at him and nodded.

"Come, then, my Pharaoh's Seer. Let us become better acquainted."

Haremakhet struggled to maintain his focus throughout the day. He felt guilty. The priests deserved better than he was giving them, but he couldn't seem to get his thoughts away from what was happening in the fountain courtyard with the priests of Bastet.

He'd asked Laqma to identify the priest that appeared to outshine the others. He'd had to be vague to ensure her suspicions weren't raised. He'd made up a story about creating another tier within the brotherhood that recognised a high priest for each of the individual gods. He felt bad for lying—it was something he'd avoided his entire life—and particularly for misleading such a gentle, innocent soul as Laqma. But it was the only solution he'd been able to think of that would enable her to use her gift of sight to pick out one priest from so many others. He prayed her gift wouldn't reveal the truth of his deceit.

As he closed proceedings for the day, he reminded all the delegates of the grand farewell banquet being held that evening. The pharaoh himself was due to give the closing speech, allowing he'd returned from his trip. As the final priest left, Haremakhet allowed his shoulders to drop and rubbed his face wearily with his hands. It had been a long and stressful three days, and the most difficult part was still to come: persuading the three priests to take the mission.

Still, he was surprised how much had been achieved in the congress itself. Although it was merely a cover story, it had delivered some gems. Many of the priests were going back to their temples with new ideas and practises that would bring the temples more in line with the everyday folk of Egypt. He hoped they'd started a movement of greater inclusion that would outlive them all but not the religion, which still faced destruction and ruin if he wasn't able to persuade the priests to put aside their lives in favour for the immortality of their religion and culture. Not an easy sell.

With a final look around the tent, he walked towards the exit in search of Laqma and her selection of the representative of Bastet.

"Your Eminence, the gods didn't talk to me about your selection process. They remained silent on the matter, but fear not. I believe this is because the selection was obvious without their interaction. There was one who stood head and shoulders above his brothers. His passion for our Lord God Bastet was overwhelming. He was pious and devoted and eager to lead the group. Your selection should indubitably be Shery." Laqma stared at Haremakhet, her eyes gleaming with earnest enthusiasm.

"Ah, I remember Shery. He is a man of great passion and vigour, but don't you feel he's ingrained in tradition to such a level that he would not adjust to change easily?" Haremakhet stroked his chin, casting his mind back to the man that had dominated the group discussions. "He seemed very conservative, no?"

"I, too, shared that concern at first, but as the gods answered his brothers' queries in often surprising ways, he accepted and embraced these sometimes crazy ideas with an abandon the others didn't share. I'm positive he's the man for the role, should you decide to implement the new structure." She looked down at her sandals, shuffling. "I thank you for this opportunity, Your Eminence. It has been an insightful and humbling day, and I believe I'm now able to comment on the value of the congress."

Haremakhet inclined his head with a laugh. "You are, my dear. Indeed, you are."

"Well, then I declare this congress to be a great idea that has enriched the lives of those who attended it and all their communities for years to come. I dare to dream of being a great seer one day, but I doubt I'll achieve even a fraction of what you've achieved in these three days. The gods asked me to thank you, and on their behalf—and my own, for what it's worth—I proffer the greatest thanks."

Haremakhet found himself strangely touched by Laqma's sentiment. "Those words are a balm to an old man's soul, my lady Laqma. Thank you for your support. I hope you'll join us for the banquet this evening?"

Laqma beamed at him. "T'would be my honour. I wouldn't miss it for anything. Thank you for the invitation. I must hurry now and start my preparations." With that, she whirled away, hurrying to begin the feminine rituals Haremakhet could but guess at.

"What do you mean? How is it possible for Kiya and our pharaoh to be so delayed? Go send out a barge with double oarsmen to retrieve them."

Haremakhet whirled away from the pharaoh's messenger. Of all the days for the wind to let him down. It was one of the dependable things on the Nile— water and wind. Now the wind had failed him. Could this day get any more tiresome?

The banquet was fast approaching, and he'd been waiting for Kiya's return before calling the candidates together. He could wait no longer, but what if young Laqma had been mistaken in her selection of Shery? He paced back and forth, throwing idea after idea away as either impractical or dangerous. He'd done everything he could to get Kiya back but so far, to no avail.

There was nothing for it. He'd need to see the men himself and convince them of the mission without Kiya's help. He'd been depending on her descriptions of her visions to sway the men but now knew they'd have to hear them from him. With a large sigh, he threw himself down on the hardwood bench and called for a slave girl to go get Shery, Nimlot, and Yuya.

The three men stepped apprehensively into the Holy of Holies, where Haremakhet had decided to hold the convocation. Only he and the pharaoh ever entered the room, so it would provide a secure meeting ground.

"Ah, my dear brothers, you must wonder why I call you here before we join our great celebration this evening."

The three men shuffled from foot to foot, wondering exactly that.

Haremakhet pointed to the wooden bench he'd pulled into the chamber earlier. "Please be seated, for what I have to say is both lengthy and heavy. A seat will make it more bearable."

They looked at each other before moving to the bench and sitting as one.

"First, may I say that I am so very grateful for you taking time to attend our congress. It has been an eventful and interesting three days. However, it is not of that I speak tonight. The congress was a ploy to bring the three brotherhoods of Sobek, Bastet, and Khepri together for a—for want of a better description—recruitment assembly."

Haremakhet cleared his throat and paced in front of the bench.

"Our high seer, Kiya, was meant to join us but has been delayed with the pharaoh. She came to me some weeks ago with a vision of such import and clarity that we were obliged to fabricate this congress to find you three men. What I am about to share with you comes from our Lord Gods Khepri, Sobek, and Bastet and can't be uttered to anyone outside this chamber. The future of our gods depends on our silence. Until now, only two people have known of what I speak, and with you three, only five can ever know of this. Do I make myself clear?"

The three priests flashed glances as each other before nodding.

Haremakhet felt beads of sweat rolling down the back of his neck. He pulled his shoulders back, looked each man in the eye, and then told them of the fate awaiting Egypt and her gods unless they took action immediately.

Yuya raised his hand, and Haremakhet nodded his

approval for Yuya to speak. "So, you are saying that each of us have been selected by our own Lord Gods to carry part of them in our bodies. To pass them on through our children's bodies and their children's bodies throughout time, until our three families can unite. That we will, in essence, provide the energy for the gods to return to full power and our beloved pharaohs and gentry to be resurrected again to form a new and powerful dominion?"

"Succinctly put, Brother Yuya. Yes. That is exactly what I'm saying. You will be the seeds of the next rising of the Egyptian dominion."

Shery jumped up and slammed his fist against the wall. "But what of our religion now? Why not work now to save it, rather than allow it to wither and die on the vine, only to await the seed to drop and hopefully grow back into full vigour? It doesn't sound like a powerful strategy. What say the pharaoh and Pabasa?"

Haremakhet walked up to him and placed a hand on his shoulder, which he shrugged off. "Calm yourself, my brother. Believe me, I share your misgivings. I have had endless, sleepless nights. I am the high priest of Karnak. It's my duty to preserve, protect, and grow our faith, and yet, the gods we serve are telling me that this will happen no matter what action I take. Only by forming the brotherhood of the House of Scarabs can we protect our gods. Anything else is a dereliction of duty. It's driving me mad, but I must trust in our gods. To do otherwise is failing in my duty."

Yuya stepped up, nodding. "I can see your predicament. I have also seen my Lord God Khepri, and I know what you say to be true. The task sounds onerous, but I didn't join the brotherhood to live in luxury. I serve my gods, and if this is the path they say I must follow, then so be it."

Shery looked from Yuya to Haremakhet. "You didn't

answer my question, Haremakhet, High Priest of Karnak. What did the pharaoh and Pabasa advise?"

Haremakhet exhaled and shook his head. "I think you'll find I did. I said just two of us know, and with you three, only five will ever know. They haven't been consulted as the gods decreed this was a decision beyond them."

"Beyond the pharaoh? The human representation of the gods on Earth? Our Lord God Pharaoh? But you speak of heresy!"

Nimlot, who had sat silently watching the three men, now stood and stepped between them. "Brother Shery, do we not know Haremakhet as one of the greatest and most pious High Priests ever to have served the pharaohs?"

Shery nodded.

Nimlot continued, "Does he stand to gain any material benefit from the action he's suggesting?"

Shery stared long at him before switching his gaze to Haremakhet. "No, he does not. But still, what he speaks of is, at minimum, high treason. How do we know false gods are not leading him from the one true path of our faith? We know they send trials to test our resolve. How do we know this is not just such a trial? He speaks without ever having seen the visions. He's basing his judgement on the vision of a foreign slave girl. Now *she* might have much to gain from the failure of our dominion."

Haremakhet acknowledged his point with a tip of his head. "That she might, but I intend to spend my entire life dedicated to the healthy propagation of our religion. You three will leave our circle, our dominion, and I will never hear from you again. But our religious practises and routines will continue unabated, and I intend to leave our religion healthier than it was when I started. They predict our dominions fall many generations from now. I fail to see what Kiya will gain from that, and I'd ask you to respect her position as the royal high seer. If the pharaoh sees fit to trust her, and the country has prospered much under her prophecies, we, too, should trust her."

Shery sank back onto the bench and put his head in his hands.

Nimlot rested his hand on Yuya's shoulder and, looking Haremakhet directly in the eye, said, "I haven't been granted the privilege of a meeting with my god, but my dreams have been riddled with visions of the fall of our empire. It's tortured my nights for weeks now. My dreams match your words precisely. I am sure it's my and my family's duty to carry this burden. So, I will accept my duty, albeit with a heavy heart to leave my home and country."

Haremakhet took his hand and then pulled him into a hug. "Thank you, brother Nimlot. I admire your courage and conviction." He turned to the bench. Shery hadn't moved and still carried his head in his hands. "And you, brother Shery? What say you?"

Shery looked up, his body carrying the weight of the world, his eyes haunted. "I cannot commit to such an enterprise without deep thought and prayer. Please grant me until the end of the banquet to find my answer. We are talking about fundamentally changing my entire life and that of my family. It warrants deep thought, no?"

Haremakhet closed his eyes, weary beyond his years. "Yes, it does, my brother, and I respect you praying on the matter. May the gods grant you the tranquillity of acceptance. Please remember this is to go no further than us. Should Kiya return, you can, of course, seek her counsel. May the gods be with you. I fear this banquet will be a trial for all of us."

CREATION OF THE GUARDIANS OF
THE ANKH

Pabasa had been supervising the kitchens and the serving staff since the congress ended. He was determined to make this final banquet a spectacle that no one would ever forget. With the pharaoh coming, it was his chance to shine, and he had no intention of failing.

The tent was refurbished with the richest carpets the country had to offer. Tables strained under the weight of the gold and silver tableware and platters of the most sumptuous food. The pharaoh's own musicians were tuning their instruments, ready to play a selection of the great man's favourite tunes, all hand-chosen by the court overseer and Pabasa. He'd left nothing to chance.

Pabasa smiled as he took one last look around the room. Soon, the brothers would arrive and muddy the perfection, so he took the time to enjoy the spectacle he'd created.

Although he'd poured his heart and soul into overseeing the proceedings in micro-detail, he'd had little hope for success of the congress outside of his events, so he was pleasantly surprised by how well the entire event had gone. Even he had taken learnings from some of the more senior priests, though he wouldn't ever tell Haremakhet. It wouldn't do to inflate his already too progressive mind. Pabasa was sure the successes came from learning from the other priests' habits, rather than the creation of lasting change.

He brushed a tiny speck of dirt from the table nearest to him and ordered the braziers to be lit. Gathering the musicians and entertainers around him, he gave a rousing speech on the opportunities facing them that night should they impress the pharaoh and his esteemed guests. He'd organised a purse for each of them if they succeeded in putting on the show of their lives. Satisfied his work was done, he marched across the temple complex, eager to change into his finest robes.

Emerging from the darkness like a spectre from its grave, one of the brothers of Bastet matched his pace and trajectory.

"Brother Pabasa, may I take a moment of your time? I have some deeply worrying news I fear I must share with you. It's a story of treachery on such a level I still can't comprehend. I wouldn't bother you on this night of celebration for anything less than treason."

Pabasa stopped in his tracks and stared at the man, speechless. He noted the perspiration dripping from the man's brow, the tightness of his mouth, and the slight shake in his hand.

"Brother, forgive me. Your name escapes my recollection."

"Brother Shery."

"Ah, yes, of course. Brother Shery, I must change my robes and return to oversee the banquet. Why don't you join me? We can talk as we walk."

Pabasa listened to Shery's story without interruption,

his heartbeat increasing with every word from Shery's lips. He scanned the temple grounds, trying to imagine this grand complex laying buried under a bed of sand for generations. The idea was so ludicrous, it bore no merit. What was Haremakhet up to? The plan seemed so devious and without obvious benefit. Pabasa scratched his head, trying to understand why they would propose it.

He felt the burn of anger creeping up, a fire in the pit of his belly. Haremakhet was failing—and deliberately so. His primary duty as the high priest of Karnak was to preserve and protect the gods and their religion. To suggest the gods would be tossed asunder and to take no remedial action was treason of the highest order.

Pabasa struggled to reconcile the action with the deeply devout man he knew Haremakhet to be. It made no sense. He would have sworn that despite Haremakhet's many failings, lack of belief was not one. He could only presume Haremakhet had been swayed to the dark side by the blonde beauty of Kiya. Her loyalty, whilst appearing strong, was not assured. She wasn't even a native of the dominion. Pabasa had argued this point when she'd been suggested as a possible replacement for the previous high seer, but her skills were so great that the pharaoh had overlooked the risk.

It seemed the sovereign was now about to pay for that oversight.

Pabasa turned back to Shery, who had watched him as he digested the story's impact. "You say you will all meet again after the banquet?"

Shery nodded.

Pabasa looked him in the eyes. "Now, my brother, your role is critical. We will stop this travesty. We will guard our beloved religion. You and I will be guardians of the ankh tonight and every night until we bring them down. You are to go back and agree to their nonsense..." Pabasa raised a hand, forestalling Shery's protests. "Don't worry. I will protect you and ensure they do not hold you responsible for your part in this. I will hide in the location and ensure I overhear everything, so make certain they repeat the full story. We will then go together to the pharaoh and blow open their deceit to his scrutiny. Do you understand?"

Shery agreed, although he voiced his apprehension at entering the enemy's den.

Pabasa swept his turquoise and gold cloak around his shoulders and hurried the man away from his villa. It was imperative that Haremakhet suspect nothing of Shery's defection. Pabasa stood in the doorway of the high priest's villa and felt for the first time that the role was his for the taking.

What surprised him was how saddened he felt. He'd long lusted after the role of High Priest of Karnak, but he'd respected and even liked Haremakhet, albeit with massive disagreements about policy and religious practises. However, the man he'd known for so many years had been a good and kind man. He felt bereaved at his loss.

Quietly, with a last look around the villa, he closed the door on both the building and his long friendship.

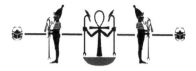

PREPARATION

Haremakhet surveyed the room. The beauty of the dancers and the strength of the wine had entranced the priests. All around him, his brothers were partying and taking opportunities to strengthen the friendships they'd built over the last few days.

It seemed the congress was a success despite its origin as an excuse to gather the houses. Haremakhet felt he would continue the practise with the other houses. So, something good *had* come from the whole mess.

Pabasa had outdone himself. Haremakhet had no doubt Pabasa's primary aim was to capture the pharaoh's eye, but despite this, it pleased him his deputy had eventually taken the cause to his heart and supported him so well. Haremakhet smiled and decided to recommend Pabasa as his successor when the day came for him to step down. He was hopeful he could help Pabasa address some of his excesses by then.

He walked around each group, sharing idle chatter whilst keeping his eye on the tent's opening. He was hoping to see the pharaoh—and more importantly, Kiya—return. Half the evening had passed, and he knew his brothers were keen to see their leader before returning to their temples in the morning.

Smiling at a group that included Yuya and Nimlot, he circled the tent, making his way to Pabasa, whom he hadn't had a moment to congratulate yet. He'd noticed Pabasa's heavy brow all evening and knew he was disappointed at the pharaoh's absence. Still, the man deserved to celebrate his success.

As Haremakhet neared him, a loud fanfare started. The pharaoh and Kiya entered behind a procession of slaves throwing fragrant petals in their path. Praise the gods, it seemed his rescue team had brought them back just in time.

Haremakhet caught Pabasa's eye, and they made their way to the podium to officiate the welcoming of the great man and his seer. No matter how many times Haremakhet met the pharaoh, he never failed to be awed by the man. It wasn't just his great height and bull-like build, or even his handsome features that made all the women swoon. It was the effortless power he exuded and the sheer agility of his mind. His mental capabilities and knowledge outstripped all his advisors'. He seemed capable of absorbing every word he heard and everything he saw. It shocked the scribes when, as a young boy, he would correct their work, having never had a formal education in the written word. Haremakhet was sure he was gods-touched and, without question, the greatest pharaoh that had ever ruled the dominion.

Tonight, he wore a short, brilliant white robe with a belt of the brightest turquoise and a golden collar studded with jewels that seemed to dance under the candle light. On his head was the double crown of both Upper and Lower Egypt, one nestled within the other.

"Brothers, please pray homage to our Lord God Pharaoh and his royal High Seer, Her Omniscience Kiya," Haremakhet announced, lowering himself to place his hands and forehead to the earth in supplication to the pharaoh. Like a wave breaking on the shore, all the priests in the tent lowered, one after the other, into the same position. Their heads remained lowered until the mighty boom of the pharaoh's voice asked them to arise.

"This pleases my heart immensely to see a gathering of the men whom I've trusted to maintain our gods' temples across the dominion. I trust this congress has proved as useful as my High Seer and High Priest of Karnak suggested it would. Kiya's shared great things with me today. I'd like to voice my appreciation for the work of Haremakhet, High Priest of Karnak and Kiya, Royal High Seer. And as Kiya pointed out, the monumental effort put into the logistics of the event by my Deputy High Priest of Karnak, Pabasa."

All the priests joined the pharaoh in stamping out their approval and appreciation. For a few seconds, the tent swayed to the beat of hundreds of feet.

"Now, apostles of the gods, please gather here in the morning for your breaking of the fast, and I will share exciting news with you. But for now, let's enjoy what's left of this fine evening. I hope to meet each and every one of you before the candles are snuffed." His words had barely left his lips before a gaggle of the more self-promoting priests surrounded him.

Kiya caught Haremakhet's eye and gestured for him to follow her to a quieter part of the tent. "Good evening, sir," she said politely as the company dictated. "I'm so sorry I missed the final day. I hope my absence didn't damage your plans. How did Laqma perform in my stead?"

Haremakhet nodded politely. "She was a delight and able to help the priests with their issues. The brethren spoke highly of her efforts, although I fear her insights for me lacked solidity. What is this news of which the pharaoh speaks?"

"'Tis but an order from the gods that I shared with him today. You will see on the morrow. I'm sorry to hear Laqma was unable to provide the gods' wisdom on the matter. So, your question remains unanswered? Maybe I could assist?"

Haremakhet watched the priests circling the pharaoh like fruit flies around over-ripe berries. "That's kind of you, but we found the answer in character observation."

"Are you two talking about the merits of the potential new High Priest of Bastet?" Laqma said, appearing at their side. "He's a fine man, don't you agree, Kiya?"

Kiya looked at her with a polite smile. "Haremakhet has yet to share your decision with me, so I'm unable to comment."

Laqma lowered her voice, "Well, should Haremakhet decide to initiate this new position, we both agreed that Shery, over there," she said, pointing towards a man in a pale green robe, "would be a fine candidate. He is pious, ambitious, and by far the most devout of the priests in my group today. It was a real privilege standing in for you, Kiya."

Laqma looked up, smiling at Kiya, whose expression had frozen as she looked into the far distance. She looked around the room with a vague expression before shaking her head and looking at Haremakhet.

"Laqma, thank you for your support today. The high priest was most complimentary about your performance. I will meet with you tomorrow to discuss your training. Now if you'd excuse me."

Haremakhet watched Kiya glide across the floor towards Shery, gathering two glasses of the fine wine from a slave girl as she traversed the floor. She handed Shery one of the glasses as he was the only man without wine within the group.

Haremakhet's heart had dropped. In that tiny shake of the head, he'd understood they'd chosen the wrong man. They'd shared the gods' prophecy with an outsider. He turned his ashen face to Laqma, who was chatting excitedly about her forthcoming training. What were they to do?

Kiya shared a toast with the group containing Shery, smiling at them as they shared the insights that Laqma had provided that day. They lamented their loss of not having spent the day with her but reassured her that Laqma had filled her shoes well. As the conversation petered out, she moved to the neighbouring group, and Haremakhet joined her once again. She chatted with the men, answering questions that Laqma had been unable to. Haremakhet noticed she paid particular attention to one tall and slender man whose name escaped him.

She watched the man as she listened to the conversation idling around her. "Your name is Subu, is it not?" she asked.

The man laughed and answered with a nod. "Oh, I fear my deeds have made me infamous. How did you learn my name?"

She smiled, her eyes crinkling in the corners. "Well, would it make you feel better if I said the gods had told me?"

His eyes widened. "No, not at all. Have my antics even reached their ears?"

She laughed. "Now I'm intrigued. Of what antics do you speak?"

Subu rolled his eyes and grimaced. "Now the high priest of Karnak and the high seer must also be party to my humiliation?"

"Well, I think that depends on the subject matter of which you speak." Kiya winked at him. "Pray don't leave us in the dark?"

All his fellow priests fell about laughing, nudging him with their elbows and encouraging to speak up.

Closing his eyes and shaking his head, Subu shared his story. "It started on the night I arrived.

One week previously.

The boat was idling in the Nile's grasp. The Lord God Shu appeared to be sleeping, for the sails were limp. Not even a breeze teased them. It had been this way for two days. Subu feared he would miss the congress if the wind didn't pick up soon.

He trailed his fingers through the water, throwing some on his face to cool his fevered brow.

"It seems unlikely we'll travel much farther today, Your Eminence," the captain shouted from the helm. "Might I suggest hiring some oarsmen? If your purse can stretch to that, it would surely help us reach Thebes in time for your meeting."

Subu sighed, loath to spend the temples coffers on himself. Yet, he saw no alternative. "Make it so, my friend. I'm feeling mighty weary, I shall retire early."

In truth, Subu had been feeling wretched for most of

the day. He couldn't stop shaking and felt the fevers burning at his brow. *This congress had better be worth this inconvenience,* he thought as he eased himself down onto the sleeping pallet and fell into a deep sleep.

He awoke to the flash of lightening and the boom of thunder immediately overhead. The boat was thrashing on impossibly strong waves that breached the hull of the boat. Lord Shu had awoken.

Subu scurried onto the main deck to find the captain and offer his help. The poor man was trying to lower the sails, but they were over-extended, and the rigging had twisted and knotted in the stormy gusts.

The captain acknowledged Subu's presence with a nod. "It's no good. I need to climb up and cut the ropes. I'll need you to follow my instructions down here."

The captain swiftly outlined his plan, showing Subu exactly what to do. Subu nodded weakly. He felt even weaker than when he'd retired for the evening, and the wave splashes and torrential rain weren't refreshing him.

The wizened old captain climbed up the mast like a monkey. He showed no fear when the waves and wind tipped the boat so that he was almost parallel to the water. Subu held onto the ropes and mast, fearful for his life. The boat righted itself, and the captain continued up.

Subu felt himself stumble, his legs suddenly too weak to hold him up. As he fell, he let go of the ropes. It all seemed to happen so slowly. The sail, free of any control, flapped, hitting the captain with such force that he had no possibility of holding on. Subu watched as the captain fell, his arms flapping wildly. He landed with a sound that reminded Subu of the splattering noise a watermelon makes when the village children throw them to the ground. The captain lay still. Unmoving. His eyes were permanently fixed in accusation on Subu.

The storm raged all night. Subu fell in and out of consciousness. He was awake when the mast snapped, dropping its entire load onto the captain's body. His eyes remained glued on the poor man as fever ravaged his own body until it again claimed his consciousness.

The sun was fearsome, beating down on him relentlessly, yet still, he could not move. His body appeared to have developed a will of its own, and it wanted to rest.

Time passed. He woke often, tortured by thirst and hunger. His clothes were soiled by the storm and nature's own urges, which would not wait. He was being consumed by weakness. Even trying to crawl across the deck seemed an impossible effort. He lifted his hand to shade his face and allowed sleep to reclaim him.

"The gods have claimed this one."

"This one's not long for the world either."

Subu lifted his eyelashes and saw a burly waterman in a stained robe standing over him.

"W...ater," he struggled to say. It came out as the merest whisper, yet the man heard it.

"By all the gods, he speaks! I'll bring you water, my brother, but first, let's get you undercover." He looked back at his companion. "Onsin, help me carry this poor man to our boat."

Subu's lowered his eyes, grateful that the gods had found him help.

Water is the humblest of Earth's resources. Yet, as it

trickled into Subu's mouth, it was glorious. He gulped, trying to force the water skin to increase the trickle.

"Take it slowly, my friend. After a long drought, you must sip, not gulp." His rescuer reached to touch his brow. "Hmm, I don't like this fever. We must fight to bring it down."

Subu nodded, sinking back down onto the pallet. "Your name?" he croaked.

"My apologies, brother. I'm Ramankh. I'm a fine boatman but lack the skills of healing. I think I should take you to the nearest town for help."

"No," Subu gasped. "Please, pray tell, to where are you travelling?"

"We're heading for Thebes, but you are far too weak to travel in a vessel such as mine with no healer."

"I have a purse. I can pay my way."

"'Tis not a matter of gold, my friend. Your life is at stake. I can't, with good conscience, allow you to travel towards your certain death."

"I've come to fear death something fearsome these days past. But if I am certain to die, it should be in the service of my Lady Goddess Bastet. Please, my friend, leave my survival in her hands, for I am one of her High Priests. The pharaoh and the high priest of Karnak have called me to Thebes on urgent business."

Ramankh and Onsin glanced at each other. "'Tis a quandary, I do profess," Ramankh said, stroking his chin.

Subu lifted his eyes to the sky and asked for his goddess's help.

The boat's cat strutted towards Subu, circling his body before climbing to rest on his chest. The beautiful tortoise shell cat looked at all three men in turn, then picked up her front paw and proceeded to wash it carefully.

"Well, may the gods strike me down. She's never done that before. She's a very prickly normally. Can you believe what you are seeing, Onsin?"

Onsin backed away slightly. "I believe I'm seeing Bastet's approval of His Emminence's plan. May all the gods bless our boat. We'll have to take him, Ramankh. It's a god-approved plan."

Subu stroked the cat's head. She rubbed her head into his hand, purring contentedly. "You're a beauty. I graciously thank you and your goddess."

The journey seemed eternal. Subu rotated between moments of total clarity and fevered unconsciousness. Both the sailors lamented their lack of healing skill but nursed him as best they could.

On the second evening, Subu lay watching the stars as his companions snuffled and snored nearby.

I don't want to die. I'm not ready.

A shadow separated itself from the other shadows and slunk towards the sleeping men. Subu was about to call out and alert his friends when the moon appeared from behind a cloud and illuminated a face.

Gliding towards him was a woman of rare, unearthly beauty. Long, thick black hair cascaded freely down her back. She wore a black and amber diaphanous robe that revealed more than it concealed. The woman knelt next to his pallet, tipping her head to stare into his eyes. Her almond-shaped eyes were the deepest green and shrouded in thick, black lashes.

She reached across the pallet and touched his brow. Her head tipped again as she focussed. She lifted her hand, her eyes staring into the distance, her fingers combing her hair in deep thought. With a nod, she rose and glided back across the boat to disappear into the shadows.

Moments later, she returned with a small vessel of cloudy white liquid. "You must drink this to lower the fires inside. It's an extract taken from the bark of a tree." She raised it to his lips and supported his head.

"But..."

"Please, Your Eminence. Drink."

Subu felt compelled to do as she asked and drank the powdery liquid.

She smiled and raised her hand to rub her nose in a circular motion. "Rest. You will feel better soon." She moved away.

"Wait, please. I don't know your name. Will I see you again?"

"I'll be close. You'll see me again. Now rest. Your body needs sleep to build energy again."

Subu felt his eyes drooping as sleep reclaimed him yet again.

Every night for the rest of the journey, she returned. Always when the others were asleep, and always just long enough to give him the potion, which lulled him into a deep and restful sleep. He struggled to remain awake so that he could find out more about her, but sleep was his jealous mistress.

Ramankh and Onsin were sure they'd nursed him back to full health and toasted their skills each night with a large beer.

"Who'd have thought two old water dogs like us would have the touch of healers? Warms the heart, it does. I reckon we'll be blessed by the gods for saving one of their own," Ramankh said for the tenth time the night before they were due to arrive in Thebes.

"My friend, we are all gods-blessed in some way in life. It's just most of us don't look for our blessings as we are too busy nursing our ills. I have no doubt you are both god-blessed," Subu said, raising his pitcher to them. "I will miss you both when I take my leave on the morrow."

"As we will you! To our Lady Goddess Bastet and her High Priest," Onsin toasted.

He didn't mention the woman's visits to them. The visits were precious, and he was frightened he may jinx her return.

He watched them sail away, the two sailors and their cat. They waved, much cheered by the large purse he'd gifted them for their troubles. Part of him wanted to continue with them. He feared that his good health and departure from the boat would herald the end of his night-time visits.

Closing his eyes and shaking his head, Subu continued. "I'd imbibed rather too much of the pharaoh's fine beer. It's far stronger than I am used to, especially after a period of such ill health. I was taking a late-night stroll around the lake, and I came upon a most beautiful woman. The same woman who'd so diligently nursed me back to health. I wanted to thank her for her help, and as a single man, I wanted to attract her attention. We sat by the lake and talked. The next night, the same again—too much alcohol and meeting my lady friend. It was innocent, you under-stand. We simply chatted about faith, principles, and honour. She was learned and bright. Only, these three meat-heads came along and disturbed us, and before I could stop her, she'd run away."

"That doesn't sound like a story of shame, my brother," Haremakhet said kindly.

"No, except these three were sober, and they swear they've seen me chatting to a black cat for the last two nights. I swear upon my beloved Goddess Bastet, I will not touch another drop of alcohol. My drinking days are over. A man who can't hold his cups shouldn't be imbibing."

Kiya's face rested into a tranquil pose before she said, "Alcohol can unlock our senses but can also limit them. Who knows which it did for you these past days?" With this, she nodded her farewells and grabbed Haremakhet's arm. "The pharaoh requires our attention, Your Eminence. Come, let's not make him wait."

"That was the third, was it not?" Haremakhet asked as they walked towards the platform on which the pharaoh sat.

"I'm afraid so. The other man is not gods-gifted. Fear not though. I have taken action as the gods suggested. By tomorrow, the problem should resolve itself. Tonight, you must keep Subu here. He mustn't return to his temple tomorrow. Come, hasten. The pharaoh looks displeased."

They hurried up onto the stage and stood on either side of the golden throne.

"Ah, Haremakhet, there you are. I beseech you to manage your deputy. He's buzzing around me like a fly around dung. He keeps wittering on about deception and intrigue. Frankly, the man's a bore. He's pompous, self-serving, and arrogant. I only tolerate him because he assists you so ably with the logistics of the temple, but I will not have him create disharmony in my court. Do I make myself clear?"

Haremakhet bowed deeply and murmured, "Yes, sire, crystal-clear. I will talk to him this very evening. I apologise. I can only imagine he's celebrated a little too hard."

"You need to watch him carefully. He's trying to discredit you and Kiya. I will not allow it. I suggest you give him a new position outside Karnak, in the remotest regions of my lands. Now I've met the over-ambitious of your brethren, introduce me to the pious and humble brothers, for in them I feel closer to my gods."

Haremakhet and Kiya bowed low again and guided him to the huddles of men at the outer reaches of the tent.

As the last men left the tent, Kiya and Haremakhet flopped down onto the deeply padded floor cushions. Kiya kicked off her shoes and rubbed her toes appreciatively. Haremakhet closed his eyes for a couple of minutes before lifting his hooded lids and studying Kiya.

"What a night—or should I say, what a few days? I'll be glad when I can return to my normal duties."

Kiya smiled a crooked smile at him. "You may be fooling yourself if you think it's over. We still need to initiate our three friends and help them build the skills to survive outside the cosseted warmth of the brotherhood. I fear our work has just begun."

Haremakhet scowled comically. "Let an old man have a few minutes of contentment before shattering his dreams, woman!"

With a laugh, Kiya stretched out across the cushions lazily. "You have a point, my friend. You have a point."

Haremakhet laughed and hauled himself up. "Come, Your Omniscience. Our friends await us. For the life of me, I know not how to handle Shery." He sighed and offered her a helping hand. "When I was a boy, I dreamed of serving my gods in peaceful piety, and somehow, I've been raised to this position, where I have less to do with religious observation and more to do with politics and policy. Now I must accept the downfall of what I hold most precious to serve my gods. I fear the world is a confusing place."

Kiya took his hand and rose gracefully from the floor. "Tonight, we include Shery in our conversations, as if he is one of the chosen, and tomorrow, the gods will ensure his silence. Do not fear, Haremakhet. The gods have a plan."

"I don't suppose you care to share the plan with me?"

"No, indeed not, for your surprise must be genuine. Now are we to meet the three tonight? I suggest we move to somewhere more private. I can hear the gang of slaves coming to prepare the tent for the morning."

Haremakhet turned and saw a small army of slaves enter the tent and begin the long process of dismantling the grandeur of the banners and bunting, the cushions and carpets, to replace them with more utilitarian trestle tables and benches. The space was being transformed from a glorious party room into a functional mess hall. They worked with such precision, it spoke much of Pabasa's relentless training and attention to detail.

Thinking about his deputy brought a frown to his brow. "I'm surprised Pabasa isn't here, crowing about the success of his planning. After all, it went off without fault, except for your tardy timekeeping," he said, winking at her.

"Well, I can hardly be blamed for the pharaoh's whims," she said, sliding her feet back into her shoes with a wince.

"Call yourself the high seer of Egypt, and you can't even foresee issues with the wind?" he said with a laugh, dodging her half-hearted swipe at him. "What do you think the pharaoh meant about Pabasa trying to undermine us? He may be a trifle bombastic and even over-ambitious, but at heart, he's a loyal man. It's not in his personality to stage my downfall, and what would he have to gain from yours?"

Kiya nodded. "T'was an odd statement, for sure. I admit

to being as baffled as you. What I can say is if he annoyed the pharaoh to that extent, he will never regain his favour. Our Pharaoh is slow to judge, but once he has, his mind can never be changed. I fear for Pabasa. His time here, even under your protection, is coming to a close. I don't need the gods to show me, for it's as certain as tomorrow's sunrise."

They walked side by side, lost in their thoughts, towards their meeting with the priests in the smallest temple in the complex.

Pabasa had tucked himself between the outer wall of the Karnak compound and the rear wall of the tiny, unused temple that Shery had told him was to be the meeting place of the priests and Haremakhet. He'd snuck away from the festivities before they ended to make sure he wasn't seen entering his hiding place.

As he waited, his temper simmered at what he perceived as his unjust treatment at the pharaoh's hand. He'd done his best to warn the pharaoh of Haremakhet and Kiya's duplicity, and yet, it was as if the great leader was deaf to his words. This man-god was the true guardian of the faith on Earth, and yet, he blew away Pabasa's concerns as if dismissing a mosquito from his royal presence.

Pabasa knew that persistence would bear fruit once he was armed with proof and witnesses. But still, the treatment rankled, especially after he'd pulled off such a grand celebration. Tonight should have seen his star ascending, yet here he was, hiding in the shadows, surrounded by dirt and cobwebs and waiting for his own leader to destroy everything he valued beyond life itself. His temper pulsed with ire.

He listened as the three priests each entered the temple, discussing the prospects of the task they'd been asked to bear. The two other priests were trying to explain that the gods themselves ordained the mission, and whilst it would prove arduous and taxing, the fact that the gods had selected them was an honour beyond all others. Pabasa raised his eyes to the skies. The arrogance of ambition seemed to have blinded them to the truth of their mission: it would result in the ending of their faith. He wanted to bound into the temple and shake them. He prayed for the strength to overcome this heinous plan.

He was completing his fourth round of prayers when he heard the gentle murmur of Kiya and Haremakhet's approach. Their footsteps seemed to drag, and with all his heart, he hoped this indicated a change of mind and course. He adjusted his position and put his ear to the small crack in the wall to ensure he heard everything that was said within the temple. He'd briefed Shery to appear hesitant, to question them and bring out the details of the entire mission. It was imperative he could take a first-hand witness to the pharaoh.

He shuddered at what he heard. Kiya outlined the supposed case for building this triumvirate. She told them of the desolate future, of the banishing of the true faith to the annals of history. Every word was treasonous and added fuel to the fire in his belly. His conviction that he would do anything to stop the House of Scarabs' formation grew with each word. No mortal could carry the essence of the gods. He knew with certainty the human body was too frail. It could only be the work of demons.

He'd found his life's purpose. He would guard the life of his religion and his country's strength and ensure nothing Kiya said would come to pass. Before the meeting ended, his cheeks wet with tears, he slid from his hiding place and scurried home to plan his next steps.

As the sun's rays crested the horizon the next morning, a fanfare of trumpets blasted across the quadrant of tents, rousing the sleeping priests. They recognised the booming voice of the great pharaoh calling the brotherhood to break their fast. All the priests dressed in a frenzy to answer his call, running from their tents to the great tent. The call had surprised Haremakhet, who answered the knock at his door some time earlier only to find the pharaoh's hand raised in his face, ready to knock again.

"My Lord God Pharaoh," he'd spluttered, dumb-founded to find the dominion's leader at his humble door.

"Come, Your Eminence. We have much to do this day. Has Kiya shared her vision with you?"

"No, sire, she has not," he'd answered, pulling his robe on and fastening the belt around his waist.

"You and I have decisions to make prior to the sunrise. Today will be an auspicious day for Egypt, for the entire dominion. Come, man, hurry!"

He'd run to keep up with the great man, and they'd reached the tent at the same moment as Kiya, who smiled and winked at Haremakhet.

"Kiya, you tease, imagine keeping Haremakhet in the dark. Do you want to tell him, or shall I?"

Kiya bowed deeply and laughed.

"I have so few pleasures, sire. Surely, you don't begrudge me my small joy in teasing His Eminence."

The pharaoh roared with laughter, his hands slapping his mighty thighs. "By the gods, I don't, but I think it's time to put him out of his misery." He turned to Haremakhet and put his arm round his shoulders, leading him into the tent. "You see, my dear Haremakhet..."

———

Haremakhet and Kiya stood flanking the pharaoh, each beaming down at the massed faces of the entire brotherhood of Khepri, Bastet, and Sobek. Haremakhet's eyes searched the tent, looking for Pabasa, who, unusually for him, had secreted himself at the rear of the tent, almost hidden behind his brothers. Haremakhet guessed Pabasa had realised he'd raised the pharaoh's ire the day previous and was keeping a low profile.

Probably a wise move, he mused.

"So, my apostles of the gods, you must wonder why I roused you so early from your slumber, especially after immersing yourselves in your cups yestereve." He stopped and allowed the weight of his words to settle. "Today is a new dawning, both literally and illustratively. The gods have demanded we share our knowledge and expand our religion beyond our fair boundaries. They have asked me to send forth masters to find and guide new followers to them." He waved his hands to include Kiya and Haremakhet in his words.

"I, as the man-god and leader of our faith on Earth, have asked the high priest of Karnak, Haremakhet, and my royal high seer, Kiya, to help me find and identify these masters from amongst your brethren. I take great pleasure in inviting Yuya, Nimlot, and Subu to step forward."

A wave of murmurs passed around the tent as the three unassuming priests made their way to the podium with wide eyes.

"Do not fear, my brothers," the pharaoh boomed with a hearty laugh. "I have nominated you three to lead your houses and to each recruit nine of your house brothers to form a thirty-strong missionary effort." He shook each of their hands before turning back to the audience of shell-shocked priests. "Do not think I ask this lightly. It will be a difficult and thankless task and take you far from the comforts and support of your motherland. However, it's a task that is gods-blessed and pharaoh-ordained, and your rewards will be great in the afterlife. Of that I can assure you.

"So, now I open the floor to volunteers. Should you wish to please your gods and lay down your life to forward our nation and our religion, please step forward and form a line behind your house leader. They and Haremakhet, with the support of Kiya, will make the final selection. I will put considerable resources forward to ensure your success in this endeavour. May our gods be with you," he said with a final flourish as he turned in a swirl of his cape and left the tent.

One by one, priests moved forward to join the visibly shocked Yuya, Nimlot, and Subu.

Haremakhet looked toward Pabasa, who was staring at him with a look of such hatred and anger. He realised Pabasa's nose had been put well and truly out of joint. Still, he couldn't worry about that now. He'd explain his inability to share the plan earlier to Pabasa, and he was sure his deputy would calm down. He always did eventually.

Pabasa turned without a backward glance and flounced out of the tent, his rage obvious to any who saw him.

Pabasa raced to Shery's tent. He couldn't believe the man had snubbed the pharaoh's personal call. He could only hope the pharaoh hadn't noticed one man's absence amongst so many others. Still, what a day to ignore the pharaoh.

Pabasa knew he needed to gather all his resources around him to convince the pharaoh of the repugnant deed being undertaken under his very nose. The red rage he'd felt in the tent returned as he saw the duplicity of their plan. To hide it within a plan that seemed to call for the faith's expansion was both genius and evil on a level he found hard to comprehend.

He flung open the tent's flap and entered. Shery was laid on his cot, breathing softly in a deep slumber. He'd slept through the fanfare and the pharaoh's call. Pabasa bent low and screamed in his ear. Nothing. Not a movement. Enraged, Pabasa shouted again at the sleeping man, who continued to enjoy his dreams, unworried by Pabasa's call.

Pabasa stared at him, a frown marring his brow. He hadn't even twitched. No man could sleep through such a shout. He shouted again. Nothing. With his fury mounting, Pabasa kicked the cot, depositing Shery on the floor in a tangle of sheets and blankets.

Shery leapt to his feet, fists raised ready to defend himself. When he saw Pabasa, he opened his mouth to protest his rude awakening. His lips moved, but no words came out. He tried again, his mouth shaping words, but no sound accompanied them. He clutched his throat, his eyes wide, and screamed—with no sound.

Pabasa watched him try to form sounds; the man had been struck mute. Pabasa clasped his arm to get his attention and calm him, and he asked him to sit on his cot whilst he went to find a temple physician. Shery's face collapsed in horror. Pabasa tried to calm him, but Shery became ever more frantic, pulling free from Pabasa to clap his hands next to his ears. Repeatedly, he clapped as Pabasa watched in confusion. Tears poured down Shery's face, and he gestured to Pabasa, shaking his index finger and pointing to his ears.

He'd lost his hearing too.

Pabasa stared at him in horror before running out of the tent and vomiting on the dusty ground. This was the demons' work. His only witness could no longer bear testimony, and without his support, Pabasa knew he was unlikely to persuade the pharaoh of the events unfolding around him. Uncaring of who saw, he sat in the dirt and cried.

THE SCHOOL

TWO YEARS LATER

Haremakhet looked around the missionary's yard. They'd achieved so much over the last two years, more than he could have dreamt. The school was built. Each missionary had been assigned a country to target and had learnt the language of the land they were to infiltrate. In just two years, they'd become proficient potters, carpenters, blacksmiths, and weavers. He was proud of them. All thirty worked with fanatical vigour, eager to pass the training phase and move out into the world to spread their message.

No one guessed the extra training the three heads of house received as they held their daily debriefings with Kiya and Haremakhet, and no one ever should.

Yuya, Nimlot, and Subu had blossomed into true leaders, which could only stand them in good stead when they went out into the world. Kiya had foreseen that tomorrow, they would be anointed as the vessels of the gods. Only then would they truly become the House of Scarabs, carrying their gods and endowed with the power of resurrection. Neither Haremakhet nor Kiya knew what the ceremony would involve, but they were confident the gods would offer illumination.

Kiya could now converse with the gods at will. It was as if a thin veil had been lifted, revealing the gods' thoughts to her. The long days of silence before the congress were a distant memory, and she was again lauded as the greatest seer to have ever lived and served the dominion. She worked diligently for the pharaoh and had helped to train Laqma until she, too, exceeded all the other seers alive or dead. Egypt prospered under their direction, and the pharaoh was envied by his neighbours.

The only cloud to blight their sky was Pabasa's perceived decline into insanity. Both Haremakhet and Kiya were certain that Shery had passed details of their mission to the former deputy high priest before being struck silent. Pabasa initially shouted about the treason of Kiya and Haremakhet, trying to find allies in the highest political and power spheres, but the pharaoh's emphatic support had quietened the mutterings. When Pabasa was posted to the dominion's farthest temple outpost, the gossip diminished.

Yuya had suggested sending Shery to Yabaktari as a support for Ahmes, whom he knew would treat the former brother kindly. Haremakhet had supported the idea and was pleased to have recently heard that Shery settled there in deep spiritual reflection. Whilst he could not communicate with the other two priests, he seemed contented. Haremakhet mourned the loss of his former deputy and the great cost the two men had paid for just learning of the gods' mission.

"Your Eminence, what brings you to our yard so early in the day? Fancy a hand at pottery?" Yuya laughed, walking up shadowed, as always, by his large black and tan dog, Merket. He thumped Haremakhet on the back with a wink.

Yuya, of all the men, had changed the most. His lean build bulked out under the hours of physical labour he did every day. He'd insisted on learning all the trades as he wanted to be in good stead wherever his journey ended. Nimlot and Subu had tried for six months but found the workload too great and quietly gave up the extra classes. Yuya was now a master potter and carpenter and more than able blacksmith and weaver. His arms rippled with muscles, and he wore an air of confidence that the leadership role had honed over the previous two years.

"How be you on this fine morning?"

Haremakhet walked towards the main school building, "Thanks for the offer, but I think my last attempt at the pottery wheel showed my skill set to be elsewhere. Where is a mystery but definitely not with clay!" he said, laughing at the memory of the misshaped pot that he'd tried to throw the previous summer.

"Praise be to the gods, please don't remind me. Now if that wasn't a fair representation of an ox swollen with babes, I don't know what it was. T'was a shame you were trying to create a cup," Yuya laughed and matched Haremakhet's steps.

Haremakhet wrinkled his nose with a huff. "Well, it wasn't that bad, but no, I'm here to see the heads of house. We need to organise the blessing of the missionaries before you leave us. Are Nimlot and Subu around?"

"Probably snoozing under a palm," Yuya said, always fast to tease his brothers for their perceived laziness. "Actually, they are both in the temple, observing silent reflections."

Haremakhet's mouth tightened at the reminder of Shery. All three of the candidates for the House of Scarabs practised silent reflection in honour of their brother, Shery, and the tremendous cost he'd paid in the formation of their mission. Haremakhet fidgeted, correcting the line of his robe. Whilst he was touched by the gesture, it added to the guilt he carried for mis-selecting Shery. If he hadn't erred, Shery would still be a high priest enjoying a normal life, rather than locked in a silent prison without means of expression.

"Let's not disturb them. We can wait under this tree for them to emerge. It will give us a chance to chat."

Both men eased themselves onto the grassy soil under the deep shade of a fruit tree heavily laden with ripe fruit. Merket circled before flopping down, his head in Yuya's lap.

"How goes it, Yuya?"

Yuya reached up and plucked a couple of the fruit, passing one to Haremakhet before peeling his own. "The men are restless to start their work and spread the word of the true gods. I'm hopeful for our faith, my friend, if the zealousness of these men is anything to go by. I'm beginning to think it's us three that are the backup, rather than the other way around. I pray this to be true." He glanced at the juice weeping down his fingers, which he presented to Merket for cleaning. "T'would be a good thing if our efforts were never needed."

"Indeed, it would, but still a necessity either way. To be honest, I'm overwhelmed at the response of our brothers. It warms my heart to see such devotion and piety. I think I shall be bereft when you go and I'm left with the political power-seekers again. I almost wish it were me leaving on the morrow."

Yuya stared into Haremakhet's eyes and reached across to clasp his shoulder. "Your role here is every bit as critical as ours. You are the firm and fair guiding hand on the helm. Without you, Egypt and our dear faith would be lost. I shall miss our chats, my friend, but I will carry the memory of them with me for as long as the gods grant me breath."

Uproarious laughter echoing from the temple's entrance grabbed their attention.

"I think it's fair to say their silent reflection is over," Yuya said with a chuckle. "After you, Your Eminence." The two men rose and brushed the dust from their robes before walking to join the two men who'd emerged into the sunlight.

Haremakhet noted that the other two men had changed far less than Yuya, but even they had a premature age to their eyes, as if they'd walked this life before. All three were quick to laugh and lacked all forms of ego, yet they carried a gravitas to their demeanour.

"Haremakhet! Greetings. How be you on this morrow?" Nimlot boomed.

They exchanged greetings and again settled in the dappled shade of the tree.

"So, what news of tomorrow? Has the pharaoh declared his intention yet?" Subu asked.

Nimlot nudged him with his shoulder. "You mean, has Kiya yet told the pharaoh of his plans?"

Haremakhet shook his head at their teasing and answered seriously. "Yes, indeed. You three are to come to the temple complex as the sun sets tonight and to stay within its boundary until the first glimmer of dawn, when you are to return for your brothers and lead them back to the temple. There, the pharaoh himself will officiate in a ceremony of blessing. Each initiate will be given his seed money and identity, and from there, they must leave the temple and the school, never to return."

"And us?" Subu asked with a slight catch in his breath.

"I know nothing yet. Fear not though. The gods will

ensure the anointment proceeds according to schedule. How? Well, your guess is every bit as good as mine. Now I must hurry. The pharaoh has asked me to attend one of his infernal luncheons with delegates from the neighbouring tribal domains."

Haremakhet stepped out from the protection of the tree, into the sun's savage rays. He looked back into three sets of troubled eyes.

"Worry not, my friends. All will be well, and come this time tomorrow, you will be on your new paths. I bid thee farewell for now."

Three sets of eyes watched him as he crossed the court-yard and left the mission. He was certain there would be much conversation between the trio.

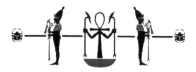

THE ANOINTMENT

Haremakhet pushed open the door to the remote chapel, then closed it behind him to hide the glow of the torches from inquisitive eyes. He jumped when he turned into the room and saw Kiya sat cross-legged on the temple floor in the middle of a swirling blue sphere. Her eyes were closed, and she seemed unaware of his arrival.

"Kiya?" he called softly.

She didn't move or acknowledge his call. She seemed to glow from within, as if she were the source of the energy that lapped and danced around the sphere. Tendrils of almost white energy forked like lightening out to the boundaries of the ball and then ran around its boundaries.

He moved forward with small, tentative steps. "Kiya, can you hear me?"

Her face, tranquil in rest, registered nothing.

Haremakhet studied her. He'd long been enamoured by her beauty and kindness, yet at that moment, her icy blue composure frightened him. It was as if she was no longer Kiya and had become something more, something omniscient and all-powerful. Still, he moved forward, raising his hand in front and tracing the form of the sphere from a distance. The tendrils followed the path of his hand, contained within the sphere, yet reaching out to him. He tensed up as he reached forward, bit by bit, until he touched the surface.

Nothing happened. The surface felt much like his water bag, malleable to touch but with a resistant pressure. He smiled. No, it was more like the yolk of an egg, contained but fine to touch.

"Kiya."

Her eyes opened, shining an emerald green pierced by amber crescents. The eyes of the gods. She pulled her hands apart as if opening curtains, and the sphere expanded, enclosing Haremakhet within its boundary. He hurried to Kiya's side.

"We have not long before the men join us. Know you the secret of the initiation, Kiya?"

When she answered, it was with the voice of four people combined in perfect synchronicity. The male spectrum was low and booming while the female voices tinkled like struck crystal.

"Welcome, our son. We have long waited to speak to you again. Today, will see the end of our mission. You have prepared the men well, and their future seems assured. Your trials are not over, and for that, we are sorry. You have served us well. We wish we could offer you peace, but that's not your destiny. We ask you to bear what the future holds, both fair and dark. Know you are the brush that paints the future of your people." Kiya raised her hand and placed it on Haremakhet's crown. "Blessings be upon you, our son, our high priest."

Haremakhet studied the expressions flitting across

Kiya's face. Sadness. Pity. Love. He smiled down a gulp and said, "My Lord Gods, I will face whatever befalls me with as much grace and fortitude as I can muster. May I be privy to the ceremony we are about to witness? What part must I play? What prayers must be said?"

"This is unlike anything you have every witnessed. We ask—and you have every right to refuse—to possess your body. We need a physical presence to pass our energy forward. Grant you our request?"

"With pleasure. You honour me with such a request," Haremakhet replied, falling to his knees.

The tendrils crept forward, wrapping around Haremakhet and pushing until he felt a presence take over his body. It compressed him into a chamber from which he could see but not contribute. He said, with no volition of his own, "It is time, my gods. We must hurry."

A tendril of energy unfurled from Kiya and separated until it formed the shining blue shape of the scarab god Khepri. Other tendrils wrapped around Kiya, merging and writhing until the translucent form of Bastet emerged, overlaid around Kiya's form.

So, I am Sobek, Haremakhet surmised.

Indeed, you are, my son, boomed throughout his mind.

The three men made their way across the temple complex to meet with Kiya and Haremakhet for the last time.

"I feel sad. I thought this would be a moment of excitement and success, but all I feel is hollow and morose," Nimlot murmured to his friends.

"'Tis true. I feel much the same but with a heavy dose of butterflies within my stomach. I'm not so much frightened as apprehensive. I realized today, stupidly late, how much we are giving up."

Yuya chuckled at his two friends' comments. He'd spent many hours meditating upon his life—past and present—and had long since come to terms with the situation. But he knew his friends were less reflective than he, so their concerns didn't surprise him.

"As we all know, this life is but a flash flood compared to the ocean of the afterlife. Think ye not of this life, and instead wonder upon the riches we'll receive throughout eternity."

Subu nudged Yuya's shoulder. "Ever the deep thinker. Do you feel no pang of anxiety?"

Yuya stopped for just a second. "Am I not human? Of course, but I temper it, knowing we carry our gods' destinies and that of our brethren past and future. It's humbling, and it tamps down my anxiety to a manageable undercurrent. We should hurry. We don't want to risk witnesses."

They hurried over the dark, unlevel ground, stumbling occasionally as they neared the cube-like structure in the farthest corner of the temple complex. Yuya felt the brush of fur against his leg. He looked down to see Merket's doting eyes staring back at him.

"Merket, home, boy!" Yuya pointed back towards the school.

Merket stared at him with a dopey grin.

"I told him to stay at the school," Yuya grumbled.

"That dog has not let you out of its sight since you first rescued it from the well. What made you think today was different?" Nimlot asked with a grin, leaning over to stroke Merket. "He knows something is up, and he will not let you stray far. I swear, he shares Kiya's foresight."

"He can guard the door and warn us of any spies, can he not?" asked Subu as Merket licked his hand in agreement.

Yuya sighed. "It seems I'm outvoted. Merket, stay. On guard."

The door opened in front of them, revealing a huge, shining ball of blue energy which gyrated around the still forms of Kiya and Haremakhet. Both were overlaid with the almost transparent forms of Sobek and Bastet. Khepri, in his beetle form, flew around their heads.

"Is it too late to change our minds?" Subu whispered. Yuya put a hand on each of his friends' shoulders, propelling them forward. The door closed softly behind them. "Guess that's a yes, then."

"Welcome. Please approach us, my children," boomed a deep, unfamiliar voice from Haremakhet's body. "My fellow gods and I thank you for accepting our mission. This sacrifice will not go unrewarded. Tonight, your bodies will meld with our energy, and your family line will forever be united with our celestial powers. But you have one final choice to make before this meld can occur. Be sure the choice is yours and only yours to give freely or decline. Whatever you choose, we will respect your wishes. Have I made myself clear?"

"Yes, my Lord God Sobek," all three men answered.

Sobek's translucent head nodded. "This last choice is the hardest and requires utter faith in myself and my fellow gods here present. We don't underestimate the depth of commitment and sacrifice it will take, nor will we lose respect should you choose to remit yourselves." He turned to study each man. He stared into their eyes for a few seconds before turning to the next, as if searching for something. With a nod, he continued, "Tonight, you must give your life in free sacrifice. You must leave this mortal realm and glimpse the afterlife. There, you must choose to return to Earth to complete your mission or to stay and enjoy the blessings of the life-ever-after. Both choices are yours alone to decide."

Subu stepped backwards, bumping into Nimlot. "You expect us to die."

Kiya stepped forward, her hands raised. The gentle, musical tone of her voice belied the weight of her words. "That is what Sobek said. Your death will be swift but not without pain. You must know the depths of your commitment and sacrifice. For us to give you the power of resurrection, you must be reborn yourselves. There is no other way."

Yuya felt the waves of anxiety flowing from his friends. He reached for them, turning them both to face him. "We knew we would carry a great burden. Our faith is strong. It is every man's destiny to die. The only difference is we know the when and the where of ours. Gird yourselves. Together, we will die. Together, we will be reborn, and together, we will be bound for all eternity via our children and our children's children. What say you?"

"I am frightened, Yuya," Subu whispered, his eyes dropping.

"As am I, my friend. As would any man of sane mind be. It is the conquering of the fear that raises our mortal souls higher and higher. Haven't I heard you preach that over and over?" Yuya said, his eyes drifting to Nimlot.

Nimlot's mouth lifted slowly until a grin broke through. With a booming laugh, he said, "Ah, Subu, caught in a trap of your own making." His wink broke the tension, and soon all three men were laughing and hugging.

"Aye. It's my choice, my Lord God Sobek and Lady Goddess Bastet. I, Subu, whilst shaking like a boy torn from his mother's arms, choose to die and face the afterlife."

"I, too, make the choice to complete my mission by dying and facing the afterlife, with this fearful kitten—no offence meant, my lady." Nimlot wrapped his arms around Subu's shoulder.

"It is my honour to represent you, my Lord God Khepri, and to walk in the shadows of the two great men before me. I choose death and rebirth to complete the meld."

Sobek broke free of the sphere and embraced each man. "Gather in a ring and hold hands. Whilst I can't make your death pain-free, as Lady Bastet stated, I can make it quick..."

As he spoke, a tendril of the energy broke away from the sphere and forked into three prongs that impaled each man before he finished his sentence.

Haremakhet watched, sickened to the stomach as all three men fell to their knees in unison before collapsing in a silent, still pile. Khepri flew from one to another of the men, resting in their open wounds and appearing to feast on their blood before vanishing with a boom.

The door flew open, and Merket launched himself at Sobek, his teeth bared. He bounced back as he hit the protective shell of the sphere. The dog attacked the sphere, growling and biting, trying to get through the membrane until he could barely move. He then settled, crying, on his master's chest.

Haremakhet had never seen a fiercer defence, nor a more pitiful cry. Merket had fought the gods to protect his man.

Yuya awoke in a soft feather bed to the symphony of snores from his roommates, Nimlot and Subu. He studied the room, curious as to his whereabouts. He spotted a jug of water on the table next to him and sat groggily, then poured himself a pitcher. The water was cool and sweet on his tongue. He tried in vain to remember what had occurred to bring him to this fine place.

His fingers ran along the fabric upon the bed. He'd never encountered something this smooth or finely woven. The room glowed golden as if bathed in the late afternoon sun, yet he saw no window or torch to illuminate it. Stretching until the knots in his back eased, he stood and walked over to the other cots to wake his friends. They had things to do. What exactly was unclear, but they needed to move.

Yuya grabbed Nimlot's nose and held it until, with a gasp and a splutter, Nimlot awoke.

"By all the gods, you rile me. Must you awaken me so? It's one of your less appealing features—this perpetual need to torture me each morning." Pushing himself up onto his elbows, Nimlot spluttered, "Where on the gods' good Earth are we?"

"Will you two keep it down? A man's trying to sleep over here!" Subu shouted at them before turning onto his side and pulling the blanket up over his head.

Yuya moved swiftly, pulling the bedding from both his friends. They leapt up, fists drawn.

"You may be the singularly most tiresome man to have ever been granted the mantle of priestdom. Why, pray tell, do you see fit to turf us from our cots so unceremoniously?"

"Look around you before you put those fists into action. Where are we?"

Both men rubbed their eyes and yawned before studying the room.

"I recognise not this room," Nimlot said, rotating on the spot. "It's not where I went to bed last..."

"My point exactly. You don't remember what we were doing yesterday, do you?"

Subu scratched his head. "My mind is somewhat blurred. I remember... well, you two. I remember that I'm a priest of the order of Bastet, yet I seem to be unable to grasp what I've been doing recently or even where I've been. This is most disturbing. I feel disenfranchised."

Yuya poured both men water before sitting on the edge of the bed, stroking his chin whilst he thought.

"I suggest we explore our surroundings and hope whatever potion we've been given wears off and restores our memories. I have a strong sense of purpose without the knowledge for what. It's a little off-putting."

The men dressed quickly, discarding their fine sleeping apparel, and hurried to the only door in the room. It opened into a long corridor dotted with rows of doors leading off from it. It, too, was lit by some magical glow. The trio eased along the corridor mutely. As one, they decided not to explore any of the rooms but to make for the wide staircase that swept down to the ground below.

As they descended the staircase, the view opened into a huge atrium. It was fitted with gatherings of chairs and couches and a heavily laden dining table large enough to hold twenty rotund individuals. Their gazes were drawn to the large window. Outside was an expanse of grasses waving in the gentle breeze, surrounded with trees of such height and breadth, they didn't appear possible.

"Can you imagine how many chairs we could make from one of those?" Yuya murmured.

"Ever the practical!" Subu said with a laugh. "Faced with trees of such exquisite beauty, you think like a carpenter."

"That's because I am one now," Yuya agreed with a

laugh. With a jump, he snapped his head around to his friend. "By the gods, Subu—you hit the nail on the head. I'm a carpenter and a priest. I'd forgotten that. But the why still eludes me."

"It will come in time. For now, I intend to enjoy this rather lovely feast laid out here. I could get used to this place," Nimlot said with a grin. He grabbed a large leg of meat and bit into it, the juices pouring down his chin and onto his tunic.

"Shouldn't we explore before eating?" Yuya asked.

"And leave this food to waste? No, not happening. My stomach would roll over and die if I left this table without filling it."

Subu looked at Nimlot quizzically. "That may be the point."

"Come, stop worrying. Join me. This food is a gift from the gods. I've tasted nothing like it before."

Yuya shrugged and sat down, piling his platter with food. "I suggest we create a plan whilst we eat. We need to work out where we are and why," he said, biting into a slice of cheese. "Blessed be this food," he said, closing his eyes to relish the flavour.

Subu joined them at the table but didn't eat. "I fear we are no longer in Egypt, for I know not any lands so lush with greenery or with trees of such resplendent height. Albeit, I have not travelled as widely as you, Yuya."

"The delta where the mother Nile spreads her fingers across the land is verdant and fertile, but even there, the trees are as elsewhere. These trees are alien to my eyes. I fear we have been taken away from the land of our birth." Yuya tipped his head, resting it on his hand. "What puzzles me is why we've been taken, yet appear to be free to wander. If prisoners, surely we would be bound and locked behind secure doors, not given freedom of this palace. Where are the guards or our hosts? Why are we alone in this vast place? It puzzles me fiercely."

"I suggest we roll this food into cloths we can carry. It may be a long journey ahead of us to return to our land, and sustenance will improve our chances. Then let's find a route home." Subu acted as he spoke, placing vast loafs, cheeses, and other less perishable foods into the middle of the cloth. He rolled it, securing it in a hoop with strong knots before placing across his body.

"What are you doing, man? I'm happy here. Leave the food be," Nimlot grumbled.

Subu ignored his protests and pulled Yuya to one side. "Yuya, help me get Nimlot away from that table. He's enchanted by the food."

Yuya gave the food one last look of longing, then grabbed pockets full of dates and nuts before helping Subu to move their friend.

They headed to the door leading outside, all the while having to pull Nimlot between them. As soon as the door opened and the pristine air hit them, Nimlot quietened.

"I know not what came over me. The food bewitched me."

"You are always bewitched by food, my friend," Subu pointed out as he marched forward into the waist-high grasses. "'Tis without doubt your greatest weakness. I'd hate to spend time with you in a famine."

Yuya laughed, ducking just in time to avoid a cuff around the head by Nimlot. "Hey, t'was not me that jested."

"No, but t'was you that laughed," Nimlot replied with a hearty chortle. He stopped as he saw Yuya's expression.

Staring behind him, Yuya's eyes were huge and unblinking, his body frozen. Nimlot turned to look and gasped in wonder. The building they'd left formed a vast wall stretching as far as the eye could see. Next to it stood a gate that towered higher than any building. Higher than ten buildings piled upon each other. The gate appeared transparent, yet it was formed from continuously running water, like a vast waterfall.

"Come on, you guys. Keep up. Oh, my..." Subu had also turned.

All three men stood with their mouths open, staring at the sight. Slowly, they moved in consensus towards the gate, stopping as the mist from gate freshened their skin.

"How can this be?"

"Where does all the water go?" Yuya asked, staring down at the thin slit at the bottom of the gate, through which the torrent seemed to disappear.

Subu looked up, watching the sunlight play on the water's surface. It bounced from wave to wave, creating a rainbow in the mists surrounding the gate. As he watched, the water twirled, creating tendrils that swirled in the gate, forming sculptural shapes. He watched the tendrils closely before calling out to his friends.

"Do these tendrils remind you of anything?"

Nimlot watched them. "Yes, the impossibility of what I'm seeing. This is frightening me. Nothing on the mortal realm can manipulate water in this manner."

"Nothing on the mortal realm, eh?" Yuya pondered. "So, something beyond the mortal realm?" As he spoke, the gates slowly glided open, revealing a woman standing in a spotlight of golden sunlight.

"Momma?" Yuya sprinted forward into the woman's open arms. He lifted her, swinging her around in a tight embrace. "Momma?"

"Yuya, my son, seeing you gives me the peace I have

long awaited. Come, please enter. There are many here waiting for you."

Yuya's cheeks were wet with tears as he pulled back to look down into the face he remembered from his youth. She smelled just as he remembered—a fresh, clean scent with just a hint of summer roses. She raised her hand to cup his cheeks before drying his tears.

"Come, my darling. I want you to meet my parents. How they long to see you. Your sister too."

"I can't remember when I last saw you, but my heart has ached for you ever since," he answered, staring into her dark eyes.

She smiled gently. "It has been more years than any mother should be parted from her son." She took him by the hand and led him into the gates.

Subu looked around. His heart was warmed by the reunion, and yet, this was wrong. It was all wrong. He ran and grabbed Yuya, pulling him from his mother's hands.

"'Tis not the time for this reunion. When the time is right, the reunion will be all the sweeter. Now is not that time."

Yuya pulled himself free. "Are you completely mad? You expect me to leave my mother after losing her for so long?"

"Losing her, Yuya? How did you lose her?"

Yuya glared at him before his face fell. "I know not... but that is of little importance, for now she is here. I will not lose her again."

Subu held his hands up in a gesture of peace but forged forward with his argument. "What if, by keeping her now, you lose her for eternity? Is that a risk you care to take?"

Yuya's mother hurried forward. "Your friend is touched by sunstroke, my son. We must forgive him, for he knows not what he is saying. Come, you are all welcome. People await you all."

Nimlot had been silently observing the situation. "Subu, your conviction runs true. Now is not the time for these reunions. How I know that, I do not understand, but of it I am certain. Yuya, this is not our path to tread. One day, maybe, but that day is not today. Come, my friend. Madam, please excuse us. Your son has work of importance to complete before this reunion can have its happy conclusion."

Yuya fought both men rabidly. "It's my choice and only my choice."

Subu and Nimlot froze. "Aye, Yuya, that it is. Make your choice," Subu whispered.

Yuya's mother wrapped herself around her son. "Make your choice, my son, and make it wisely. I will love you whatever you choose. The question is, will you love your-self? Choose."

Yuya slowly pulled his arms free to wrap them around her. Holding her gently, reverently, and looking down into her sweet face, he remembered so many happy times. Every memory was wrapped in a veil of deep love that would tran-scend time and distance. He smiled, studying every aspect of her face before pouring kisses upon her.

"I must go back. My choice is to go back. I love you, Momma, but now is not the time. Keep a space ready, for one day, I will return most joyously."

She nodded, her lips curling into a gentle smile. "There is a place in my heart for you that is always warm and loving. I will wait a little longer for you. Now hurry, my son..." she said, pointing back into the meadow, "for your destiny awaits you."

Yuya closed his eyes, hugged her tight, then took a huge breath and released her to join his friends.

"I am proud of you, my Yuya. As proud as a mother can be. Farewell to thee for now."

He turned towards the meadow and saw a man watching them. All three walked towards the man, who was surrounded by a halo of blue energy. They walked silently in a line, three men walking as one.

"You have returned?" the man asked, watching them with an unsettling intensity. "Have you made a choice?"

Subu smiled. "I was untested."

The man shook his head. "There was nothing to test. Your fear of death was the only barrier to your choice. There is nothing you want more than completing the mission. Your choice was already made, my son. You remember everything now, do you not?"

Subu nodded. "I do, and I choose to return."

The man turned to Nimlot and Yuya. "What say you two? With no memory of your past, have you made a choice? Will you remain here or return to face your destiny?"

"Who are you to ask us what we choose?" Nimlot demanded. Subu gasped whilst Yuya chuckled.

The man threw his head back, and a laugh as loud as thunder rumbled around the meadow. "You, Nimlot, always make me laugh. We chose well with you three. I do believe you will keep us entertained for many years to come, as will your children and their children." With a huge wave of his arm, the man transformed into Khepri, his body intact but his head taking the form of the scarab beetle.

Nimlot leapt backward. "You looked much better before." Yuya and Subu both gasped this time, spluttering their apologies to the god.

Khepri merely took the form of the man again. "I look better and can talk. This is my favoured form, but unfortunately, I can only hold this form here. 'Tis a nuisance but one I bear. Now I will have your decisions, for the gods await us."

Yuya stepped forward and knelt before Khepri. "My Lord God Khepri, I am bound to thee. I choose to serve thee as long as my life lasts and to fulfil my destiny in doing so."

"Stand, Yuya, my son. I accept, most happily, your choice." Khepri turned to Nimlot. "Well, my friend of the loose tongue, what is your choice?"

"I'm most terribly sorry, My Lord God Khepri. I fear my mouth often works before my mind. I meant no insult or offence."

Khepri grinned at him. "Think nothing of it. I thank you, in fact. I have lived an eternity, and there is little I haven't heard, but never in all that time has someone insulted me to my face. I find it refreshing and amusing. I look forward to sharing it with the gods."

Nimlot groaned. "Could I persuade you not to mention it to my Lord God Sobek?"

"No. No, you couldn't. For he, most of all, will find it amusing. He'll enjoy your courage. So, what is your choice?"

"If I stay here, will that mean I never have to face Sobek?"

"No."

"I didn't think I'd be so lucky. My choice is to follow my destiny in service to my gods, runaway mouth allowing."

The meadow shook with the force of the pressure wave that bore across it from the blue sphere that entrapped the three men and Khepri.

Haremakhet continued to watch the bodies, unable to do anything else whilst Sobek controlled his body. Many minutes had passed, and the bodies had not taken a single breath. They appeared quite dead. Merket continued to nestle into Yuya's body, crying piteously.

Sobek and Bastet roused themselves and moved over to the bodies. They arranged them onto their backs in a circle, with their heads pointing to each other's, their hands joined, and their feet pointing out. Merket's lips rolled back, and his teeth latched onto Bastet's arm before the barrier went up. Bastet fought to fling the dog away, only succeeding by beating the dog's head against the thick stone wall. As Merket released his grip, the barrier rose, keeping him away from her. Bastet held Kiya's arm, nursing the wounds that bled onto the compacted soil floor.

Sobek seemed amused by the antics of the dog as he leaned down to heal the head wound Bastet had inflicted. When he turned back to the trio, Haremakhet saw a blue glow emanating from their hearts, visible through their fabric clothing. The glow rose up their chests and necks until all three mouths opened and a blue scarab beetle scuttled out of each. The beetles rose as one, flying around the three bodies as if sucked upwards in a funnel. As the beetles flew ever faster, they blurred, forming one large, glowing blue beetle the size of an eagle. It settled between Sobek and Bastet.

Sobek watched the three men intently, allowing Haremakhet to see them gasp as life returned. Their skin gradually blushed with the flow of blood, and the three men struggled to sit up.

"Rest, our sons. Rebirth can be trying on the body. I and

my fellow gods wish to thank you for your choice tonight. There is but one final element of the anointment to undertake. You must take our bodies into yours." Bastet smiled as all three men looked at the gods in horror. "Fear not. This part does not hurt. Khepri, I must warn you to approach Yuya with care. That mongrel does not take kindly to people near his master. He's fought two gods already to protect this man." She showed her bleeding arm. "Whilst dogs are not my natural friends, I find this fellow's loyalty admirable, if a little misguided."

Yuya starred at the black dog with tanned paws. "'Tis my fault, not his. If I'd introduced you as friends, he would not have attacked. I left him on guard." Yuya pointed at everyone in the room. "Merket—friends. At rest."

The dog rolled over and showed his belly with a grin, his tongue lolling out.

Sobek stepped forward to help Nimlot to his feet. Bastet offered Subu her good arm. Yuya scrambled to his feet as Khepri stepped forward. The sphere expanded around them, the blue energy swirling and curling like mist in wind. From each god, a tendril of the palest blue flowed, moving towards the priests. As they neared, the tendril flattened at the end, forming a flat platter on which a miniature version of the god appeared, no larger than a grape. Each god offered their priest this tiny offering.

Yuya was the first to reach forward to take the offering. He took the tiny scarab beetle in his hand. It rose on its rear legs, watching him before sinking painlessly through his palm. He saw its passage under his skin, a blue glow working its way up his arm.

Subu took the tiny cat and Nimlot the crocodile. Each statue disappeared into their hands before working up their arms to disappear.

Bastet and Sobek joined hands with the trio, Khepri and Merket in the middle.

"Now, my children, close your eyes," Sobek's booming voice ordered.

The men's hands were dropped. The temple was empty except for the three of them and Merket. They opened their eyes and looked to each other, studying eyes changed forever to a striking emerald green curtained with amber crescents.

They heard words echo around the temple, though no mortal mouth uttered them.

"Welcome to the House of Scarabs."

DESTINY

The pharaoh can't be accused of saving his gold on this event, Pabasa mused. Staring around the stadium erected to allow the pharaoh's subjects to participate in the blessing and the large celebration, Pabasa felt his rage bloom again. Not just at the injustice that had been served against him but at the public mockery of his faith and his pharaoh. They would pay. He'd extract payment from the souls of Kiya and Haremakhet for what they'd done to him, to Shery, and to their faith.

Pabasa studied the stadium, looking for the perfect vantage point from which to act. He carried on sweeping the floor as he peered out from under his beggar's cloths, observing, plotting and seething.

"Are you ready, my dear?" Haremakhet asked from behind Kiya.

"As ready as one can be on so little sleep, Your

Eminence," Kiya replied, smoothing down her diaphanous robes. "I shall miss them fiercely."

"As will I, my dear. Come, the pharaoh awaits us..." he answered, pulling the canvas flap to one side.

"Wait! Just a moment, my friend." Kiya stared beyond him into the open arena, with its towering stadium sides. Her eyes glazed, her expression serious.

Haremakhet watched without comment, content to wait for her to share her latest vision. Her eyes cleared as she focused on him. Her face was carved from marble, expressing nothing. She shook her head lightly and smiled.

"I'm ready, my dear Haremakhet. Our long journey is almost over, and I can't think of a better companion than you. For that, I thank you."

"You don't wish to share the latest vision?" he asked.

She shook her head with a serene smile. "'Tis not a vision to be shared with you, Your Eminence. T'was purely for my consumption. Shall we?" She gestured towards the tent's exit.

He took her hand and bent low to kiss it. She, in turn, placed a chaste kiss on his cheek before leaving the confines of the canvas canopy. They raised their hands in welcome, and a roar of approval shook the arena.

They joined the parade of the pharaoh's royal guard walking across the arena to the ceremonial podium in front of the massed gathering of the pharaoh's subjects. The crowd cheered and jostled for the best position to catch a glimpse of the famed high priest and high seer. The wooden structure rang to the sound of stamping feet and whoops from the crowd.

As Haremakhet and Kiya mounted the steps to the podium, a fanfare echoed around the space, and an orator announced their arrival. Taking their seats to the right of the pharaoh's grand throne, they acknowledged the outpouring of love from the gathered masses.

"'Tis a sight that warms my heart, to see the people so included. We've come far, Kiya," Haremakhet said whilst waving at the crowd.

"Indeed, and solely because of you, Your Eminence. Today is your day and sanctioned by our gods. We must not forget that."

"Shall we call forth the missionaries?"

"Yes. It is time."

Haremakhet nodded at the master of the ceremony, and the orator's voice boomed out.

"We, the children of the gods, call forth their beacons of faith. The good men who will carry their names out into the heathen lands and bring the enlightenment we enjoy to a larger audience. Come forth, missionaries of the gods. Present yourselves."

Gates in front of the podium swung open, and there stood three ranks of men behind their leaders.

"Welcome, House of Bastet. Please enter this sacred assembly."

Subu raised his banner depicting the goddess Bastet and marched into the arena, followed in formation by his nine brethren. They stopped just a chariot's breadth from the podium.

"Welcome, House of Sobek. Please enter this sacred assembly."

The crowd roared its approval as Nimlot raised his banner and walked forward with determination, leading his men to stand next to Subu.

"Welcome, House of Khepri. Please enter this sacred assembly."

The crowd became deafening as Yuya lead his men

forward. He'd grown popular and had earned the respect of the people of Thebes by volunteering his new skills to help the poor. He'd worked tirelessly in his limited free time to support Haremakhet's inclusion programme. There wasn't a family that his kindness hadn't touched. He raised his hand, acknowledging the crowd's roar before joining the other two houses.

Haremakhet nodded at the ranks of men and raised his hand to the master of the ceremony.

"Be stood for our Lord God Pharaoh—blessed be he."

A guard of one hundred soldiers clad in their ceremonial outfits lined the gateway into the stadium and in front of the stalls. A fanfare sounded in waves around the stadium. The crowd were silent, eager for a view of their god on Earth. A pounding rumbled around the stadium like a heartbeat, growing louder and louder, until a golden chariot pulled by two white stallions swept into the arena.

Driving was the pharaoh, dressed in white and adorned with chokers and amulets of dazzling gold. He steered the chariot around the stadium three times before pulling to a stop at the base of the podium and leaping down from the rear.

The crowd burst into voice, screaming his name. He smiled and turned to them with a hand on his heart and a fist raised to the skies. All eyes were on him.

Haremakhet walked forward to welcome him. Kiya leapt forward, blocking his path. She swivelled in mid-air and fell, clutching her neck. No one noticed. All eyes were on the pharaoh. Haremakhet crouched down and tried to pull Kiya's hand from her neck.

"No, my friend. 'Tis too late for me. My time has expired as the gods willed. The ceremony must continue. Cover for me—pray tell I've fallen unwell."

Haremakhet stared at her, his eyes heavy with unshed tears. "No, my little seer. 'Tis but early in the day for you. This cannot be."

"I foresaw this. If I hadn't moved, t'would be you, and your work is still undone. Mine is done at the temple. Fear not, Haremakhet. I am content with my lot. I thank thee for your friendship these years gone. Now do me the respect of following my last request. Gather the pharaoh, for I must share my final vision. You will be safe. The killer has left the arena. Please, Haremakhet, hurry. My energy fades."

Haremakhet stroked the hair from her temple and nodded, tears rolling down his cheeks. He rose as a weary old man and made his way down to the pharaoh, whispering in his ear. The pharaoh spun around and sprinted up the steps, dropping to his knees next to Kiya.

"My Lord Pharaoh, do me the honour of lifting me in your arms and placing me in my chair. The gods have willed this, and the ceremony must continue. 'Tis critical for Egypt's survival."

"My little Kiya, what have they done to you?"

"It matters not. My time is running short. Please, my Lord, do as I ask."

"Egypt cannot survive without you at my side. You have created our prosperity. You, Kiya, are Egypt. Please don't leave me," he murmured as he lifted her so gently and carried her to her high-sided chair.

"My Pharaoh, I leave not you or Egypt. You leave me. Place markers in my stead, for I hope one day to walk this mortal plane again. Laqma will be a great seer. In her hands I put you, my Pharaoh." She raised her shining blue eyes to meet his. Her hand skimmed his red hair, and she smiled. "You are a great man and will be remembered as such, but more, you've been a great friend to a poor slave girl. Farewell, my Amenhotep."

Kiya's eyelashes fluttered and fell for the last time.

Haremakhet felt his breath catch and a chasm open inside his chest. She'd gone. He was alone. Alone to carry out their task and to make her death meaningful. His hand hovered above the pharaoh's shoulder before falling to rest lightly on it.

"May she enjoy the full bounty of the gods," he whispered. "My Lord, come. We must grant her final wish. We owe her that much."

The two men stood side by side, united by an overwhelming grief and the burden of duty. Haremakhet heard the pharaoh take a deep breath before turning to the crowd, which had become restless. He raised his fist in the air, punching the air three times. Haremakhet instructed the master of ceremony to repeat the fanfare. The crowds roared their appreciation. Haremakhet knew the crowds were too far away to see Kiya clearly and decided to leave her seated until the ceremony concluded. In some small way, it pleased him that she could be present for this final step in their plan.

He looked back at the missionaries and saw the tears washing Yuya's cheeks. He knew he'd witnessed it all.

Much of the ceremony was a blur. Haremakhet remembered the roar of the crowd's delight. The strength of the men's voices as they'd said their oaths. The smell of the horse's adrenalin. The sad and brief farewells murmured to Nimlot, Subu, and Yuya as they led their men from the grounds into a new life. Merket, as always, shadowed Yuya.

He looked up at the pharaoh's voice.

"I will have the man responsible for this. May the gods smite me if I don't. He will suffer a most unpleasant death and be denied funeral rites. I will not allow him to access the heavens and bother Kiya again." His voice shook with fury, yet his hands were so gentle as they picked up Kiya. He cradled her in his arms, looking down at her face, so peaceful in death. "Is there a back entrance to this podium? I don't want her paraded in front of the people."

Haremakhet nodded and led him down the stairs in the back of the podium and to the tent he and Kiya had left so recently. He watched as the pharaoh laid Kiya onto a lounger, adjusting her clothing and hair until she appeared to be resting.

"What will we do without her, Haremakhet? You know as well as I, she was the strength behind my crown. My strongest weapon and my kindest council. How can I reign without her?"

"I know not, my Lord. However, I trust in her, and she said we would be fine, so in that we must draw comfort."

"In her honour, I will construct stones and plaques dedicated to Khepri across the dominion. May he aid her resurrection and return her to us."

"May I suggest one next to the great lake? I know it was her favourite place to contemplate. I think she'd like that."

The two great men of Egypt dropped to their knees, incanting the prayers of the *Book of Death* as tears washed their cheeks.

Haremakhet sat with his knees crossed in front of the podium, squinting up at the large scarab that topped the memorial. He'd sat in this exact spot across from Kiya, chatting about the mundane humdrum of daily life so many times previously. He was happy with the placement of her memorial. The pharaoh had been true to his word and had created countless memorial plinths and stones across the country depicting Khepri, the God of Rebirth. All were dedicated to the memory of Kiya, Egypt's greatest seer.

EPILOGUE

Yuya stopped to mop his brow. Scything in the heat of the day was tiring in the extreme, but he needed to get the crop harvested and stowed away before the desert sands blew in on the deadly winds. His eyes crinkled as he looked into the distance, studying the amber glow on the horizon. It was moving in fast.

He shouted for his sons and wife to come and help gather the crop he'd cut from the ground. The family worked tirelessly, united in purpose. They picked the last stems just as the winds whipped their clothes and the sand grains struck their faces.

"Hurry, Yuya. We must batten down the house before the storm hits," his wife urged.

He nodded, about to turn, when he saw something on the horizon.

"Can you see that figure in the distance, wife?"

"Aye, 'tis no business of ours. Come, let's go," she screamed into the wind, her words carried away from them.

"I must help. We can't leave a soul to get lost in the storm."

Agila stared at him, shaking her head. "And what of your family? What of securing our home?"

"Get Tutanpet to aid you. Hurry, woman. You secure the house. I'll take Gibil and bring the stranger to shelter from the storm with us. Hurry!"

Yuya leapt onto Gibil's back and urged her forward, towards the distant figure. Gibil, although advanced in years, galloped across the land, heading straight towards the oncoming wall of airborne sand. They covered the distance, buffeted every step by the winds and sand.

Gibil struggled, as they met the storm, to maintain her speed. The figure moved with ease towards them, as if untouched by the desert wind. A woman dressed in pristine white, her head uncovered. As they neared, she raised her golden head and smiled.

Kiya.

Yuya almost fell from his trusty mount. Kiya was dead. He'd seen it with his own eyes so many years before. Taken by a poisoned dart. He'd heard news that the royal court had tried Pabasa for the crime in absentia. Although, the man had disappeared. Despite a dominion-wide search, he'd vanished without a trace.

Kiya?

Leaping from the saddle before Gibil stopped, Yuya ran towards her.

"What's this before me? Are my eyes playing a cruel trick? Your Omniscience?" He fell on his knees before her.

"What is this, Yuya? Rise. Are we not friends?" she answered with a dazzling smile. "My eyes are happy to fall upon you after all these years, my friend."

"But you're dead..."

"Come—are you, of all people, shocked by a resurrection? You, who carry the power to do so?"

"Kiya?" he whispered, rising and taking her hands in his, "it's really you?"

Her cornflower blue eyes gazed into his, and she smiled. "It has been too long, my friend. 'Tis better than I can express to see you again."

He held her hands and noticed fine creases next to her eyes and streaks of grey in her hair.

"You have taken so much longer to find than the others. Yet, you've left legends behind you. I've heard tales of a man so strong, so kind. You've exceeded the gods' expectations."

Yuya noticed that they were unaffected by the storm, which raged around them, throwing sand, branches, and stray materials with a fearsome velocity. Yet, the storm didn't touch them. The air in a sphere around them was still and silent.

"You've seen the others—they survive? Tell me everything."

Kiya's eyes saddened. "Subu and Nimlot flourish. Nimlot moved into the Northern climes. He has a fine family and is entrenched and appreciated in his new community. Subu was more transient and has yet to settle. He's covered great distances but has witnessed some fearsome battles, escaping the grips of Pabasa's group."

"Pabasa survives?"

"Yes—and prospers. He's someone to be feared, Yuya. He's created a group self-styled as the 'Guardians of the Ankh'. They have found favour with Akhenaten, the new pharaoh. They are well-funded and trained killers with just one purpose— your death and that of your brothers in the Houses of Sobek and Bastet."

Yuya absorbed her words. "You've said nothing of the other missionaries."

She bowed her head, her bottom lip covering her top one. "Alas, they've not been so lucky. To my knowledge, only three have escaped the net of the Guardians. Once caught, they are executed and denied a proper burial."

Yuya swallowed down the bile that rose at the thought of the loss of such good men. Men he'd trained, befriended, and led.

"Yuya, I can't explain how sorry I am to be the bearer of such sad news. We did not foresee this outcome. I wish I'd known as I'd have tried to save them. T'was not to be. The gods have promised to grant them great privilege in the afterlife. It's not much consolation, I know, but it's all I have."

Yuya nodded slowly, his mind lost in a thousand shared memories of his lost comrades.

"I am happy to see you for sure, Kiya. But I fear your visit is not a social one. What say you?"

"'Tis true. I have left my family to come on this pilgrimage to find you three members of the House of Scarabs. My time on this plane is limited. I will fall again, for a final time, at the hand of Pabasa. In doing so, I will take his soul with me. This will not end the Guardians of the Ankh, but it will give you a respite from their focus. You must take your family north, across sea, land, and sea to an island of angels. That will be your family's safe place. Before you leave our dominion, you must take two of the memorial plaques dedicated to me upon my earlier death. Those must form part of your home in this new land, for without those plaques, you will not be safe."

"I am settled here, Kiya. Can I not protect myself here, where I have family and friends?"

Kiya's eyes glazed, and she stared into the distance, unmoving.

She turned to him and raised her eyes to his, eyes transformed to green with amber crescents. "If you do not heed our warning by the next harvest, this land will run red with the blood of your family and friends. Sell this land and move, our child. Take your family and create a new life. You must not fail, for you carry our strength." Her eyes returned to their blue hue, and she shook her head.

Yuya nodded, his lips tight. "'Tis settled then. I move on."

"Yuya, this will be a journey of generations. You will not see this land of angels, nor will your son, but one day, that is where your descendants will settle. You must school your children and grandchildren on this mission."

Yuya nodded, stroking the head of Gibil as he pondered Kiya's words. Kiya laughed.

"Don't tell me! Is this Gibil, alive and well?"

"One and the same. My loyal friend through many an adventure."

"And what of Merket, the god-fighter?" she asked, rubbing her arm.

A shadow crossed Yuya's face. "Alas, I lost him two summers ago, but I have his daughter and a host of grandchildren under my feet. He was an exceptional dog, loyal and steadfast, and his family all share that characteristic."

Kiya smiled. "To call one Haremakhet, my friend! Is this in honour or jest?"

Yuya laughed. "I'd forgotten nothing escapes your knowledge. Yes, I have Haremakhet and Kiya. Kiya is the mother of the clan. Both were named honouring my dear friends."

"Kiya as well? That I did not know," she answered with a laugh.

"Haremakhet should go with you to offer protection."

"Protection for my daughter, not me, but yes, I would appreciate the companionship as I make my way home for the final time. Thank you."

The storm outside their sphere was easing, and Yuya gestured towards his house.

"Please come and meet my family and break bread with us. Your return can wait an evening, can't it?"

She nodded with a beam. "I'd like that. Thank you."

They chatted as they ambled back towards Yuya's land.

"I married too, Yuya. My life has been peaceful, and I was blessed with the birth of a daughter," Kiya said. "I'd prayed to all the gods that they would save her from carrying the burden of foresight, but sadly, the gods didn't answer my prayer. I'd hoped for an easier life for her."

"Ah, but the sight is surely a gift too, is it not?" asked Yuya with a frown.

"It can be a gift, but it can make you a valuable asset to be acquired by the powerful." She kicked her heels in the dirt. "The gods have promised me that Aylaya will only ever serve you and your brothers. For that, I am happy."

Yuya pushed the door open and guided Kiya inside, leaving Gibil free to roam the land. Shutting the wind out, he turned and introduced his family to their esteemed visitor. The dogs barked furiously at the stranger in their midst, except for the gangly form of Haremakhet, who nuzzled into her skirts.

"Family, I'd like to introduce an old friend of mine, Kiya. Come forward and greet my friend."

Kiya looked down into four faces ranging in age from three to fourteen years old. Four boys. Four faces topped with rich, red hair and eyes of the greenest hue, each bracketed with amber crescents. She was toppled into one of her visions.

A young woman with the same face, red hair, and shocking eyes twirled out of a doorway into an old man. Papers flew everywhere. The woman and a dark-haired man bent to help retrieve the papers, and as the three reached for the same papyrus, their hands touched, and the blue sphere of the gods surrounded them.

The House of Scarabs would survive. Her mission was complete.

THE END

I hope you enjoyed my little tale. As an indie author, I totally depend on reviews to encourage other readers to take a chance on my books. I'd be so grateful if you'd spare a moment to leave one on Amazon. It just takes a moment and makes the world of difference to me. Thank you.

If you enjoyed this book consider checking out other books in the series:

Books in the House of Scarabs Series

Genesis - Prequel
House of Scarabs - Book 1
House of Resurrection - Book 2

FINAL THOUGHTS

Sometimes, when you are writing a historical novel, you have to let the story guide you. This means historical facts take second place to narrative and plot. In the most part, I have tried to stay true to the period.

Again, I feel my muse has guided me rather well, as many of the story points I wrote, without any prior historical reference, turned out to be historically correct. I'd decided that the pharaoh would be Amenhotep III, father of Akhenaten, the pharaoh who turned his back on the gods to follow one god, and grandfather of Tutankhamun.

It was only later, after I'd written the scene of Kiya's

memorial stones and the scarab plinth, that I found out he was the pharaoh who created these monuments to Khepri. A happy coincidence or a fact stored in my subconscious? I prefer to think that maybe the gods granted me a moment of Kiya's foresight.

I have chosen to use the more commonly known names of places, such as Thebes, to help a modern audience place the settings.

This is a work of fiction, and for me, story takes precedence. I hope that doesn't lessen your pleasure.

The bookworm in me loathes typos or story inconsistencies, so I've worked day and night to catch the little blighters. I've set traps to find and eradicate those tricky little spelling mistakes and grammar goofs, but if you come across any, please let me know, and I will zap them with my magical editing wand. Email me at: contact@hazellonguet.com.

Thank you for using your precious time to read my book, and I truly hope we meet again in the pages of another story or via one of my social media connections.

You can follow me on Facebook:
www.facebook.com/HazelLonguetAuthor

You can tweet me at: www.twitter.com/HazelLonguet

Join my reader community:
www.hazellonguet.com/communitylp

Or visit my website and blog: www.hazellonguet.com

ACKNOWLEDGMENTS

Writing is a very solitary endeavour, and yet, no novel can make it to publication without the touch of numerous individuals.

Thanks to my amazing editor, Coral Coons of Rosebud Editing, for her patience and gentle support. Any mistakes are resolutely mine.

My parents, sister and brother-in-law have been my biggest supporters and cheerleaders. Without them, I don't believe my books would have ever be finished.

Laura, Max, Toby and Ben. Thanks for always bringing me down to earth by demanding an aunt rather than an author. Love you guys.

Merli, my writing buddy and office partner. The best Rottweiler in the world. Rottweilers are amazing dogs, loyal, loving, steadfast and unfortunately massively misrepresented in the media. He's a big softy and melts my heart when I'm busy typing a scene and he rests his head in my lap, wanting nothing more than my attention. Rescue dogs are called this because they rescue the humans they move in with – that's a fact.

My advanced reader team have been great and I owe them a debt of gratitude.

Every reader who has reached out to me with words of encouragement or written an enthusiastic review - thank you. Your words feed my creative energy and warm my soul.

Finally, thanks to you for reading my book.

HOUSE OF SCARABS

SEQUEL TO GENESIS

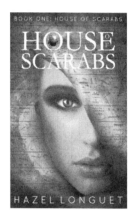

THE GODS OF EGYPT HAVE SLUMBERED FOR MILLENNIA - RELEGATED TO OBJECTS OF MYTH. THAT'S ALL ABOUT TO CHANGE...

Loner, Ellie wants a quiet life, but the gods have other plans. She's been given a choice - death or quest. Bound by the deities to two strangers (Ben an archaeologist and Gerhard an elderly scholar), the trio's lives depend on them coming together as a team.

To earn their freedom, they must uncover long lost

secrets to unlock an ancient prophecy which is protected by "The Guardians of the Ankh", a ruthless and cunning assassins' guild.

Sent on a wild chase across the desert plains of Egypt, they must stay one step ahead of the merciless, cold-blooded killers determined to ensure this unknown prophecy does not come to pass.

Will the trio succeed and unlock the gods' prophecy or die trying?

And more importantly... should they?

Available now from Amazon in ebook, paperback and large-print formats.

HOUSE OF RESURRECTION

HOUSE OF SCARABS SERIES: BOOK TWO

THE MUMMIES HAVE RETURNED.

All over the world, in museums and private collections, the mummies have resurrected. No one knows why or how. Except the Vatican & it's determined the secret shall never be told.

Now, held by curious governments, the ancient Egyptians are nothing but laboratory guinea pigs - helpless and frightened in this strange new world.

Only three people can help them; the three that resurrected them, Ellie, Ben and Gerhard.

Determined to maintain their monotheism power-base the Vatican hires a deadly assassin, The Phantom.

Now it's a race for survival and freedom.

Available now from Amazon

Printed in Poland
by Amazon Fulfillment
Poland Sp. z o.o., Wrocław

66218753R00087